Mary Botham Howitt

The two Apprentices : a Tale for Youth

Mary Botham Howitt

The two Apprentices : a Tale for Youth

ISBN/EAN: 9783337024444

Printed in Europe, USA, Canada, Australia, Japan

Cover: Foto ©Andreas Hilbeck / pixelio.de

More available books at **www.hansebooks.com**

THE TWO APPRENTICES.

𝔄 𝔗𝔞𝔩𝔢 𝔣𝔬𝔯 𝔜𝔬𝔲𝔱𝔥.

——◆——

BY MARY HOWITT,

AUTHOR OF "STRIVE AND THRIVE," "SOWING AND REAPING,"
"WORK AND WAGES," ETC. ETC.

NEW-YORK:
D. APPLETON & COMPANY,
443 & 445 BROADWAY.
M.DCCC.LXI.

CONTENTS.

—◆—

PART I.

———— ◡ ··

PART II.

THE TWO APPRENTICES.

CHAPTER I.

MAY-FAIR DAY AND THE GOOD MISS KENDRICKS.

IT was in the merry month of May, and the sixth
day of the month; the sun shone warm and bright,
and diffused a spirit of cheerfulness over the leafy
woods and the richly pastoral country that surrounded
the pleasant little town of Uttoxeter, or Utceter, as it
was, for the sake of euphony, commonly called. The
cuckoo had been up shouting for hours in the hedge-
row trees of the little convenient crofts, full of grass,
and enclosed with tall hawthorn hedges, now in full
bloom, which environed the town; and the blackbird
and the throstle were singing with all their might in
the abundant gardens, which intersected or lay behind
almost every house in the town. At six o'clock in
the morning, all that little town was astir, for it was
the morning of May-fair—an important day, for
Utceter being, as it were, the metropolis of an exten-
sive pastoral and farming district, its spring and
autumn fairs were attended from both far and wide.
The roads leading to it from all directions had, the
preceding day, been filled with herds of cattle and

droves of sheep, and long trains of horses. Yellow
and green caravans, containing wild beasts and jug-
glers, and fire-eaters, had driven through the neighbouring villages, giving to their inhabitants a
foreknowledge of some of the wonders and attractions
of the Fair. In the market-place of the town itself,
all had been stir and bustle for four-and-twenty
hours at least, and the inhabitants of the market-
place shops declared it to be their opinion, that the
people, with their booths, and stalls, and caravans,
had been up and busy the livelong night. And it did
look like it; for when, on that morning, they ventured their night-capped heads between their window-
curtains for a peep, the whole open space was full of
booths and stalls; and here was to be seen the tall
sign-post of " Thomas Rigley, licensed dealer in stays,
from Whitechapel, London;" and here, " James Ford,
cutler, from Sheffield ;" there, " Morgan O'Grady,
the celebrated worm-doctor ; " and beyond, " Jonas
Solem, shoemaker, from Stafford," close by the side
of " Aaron Tagg and Son, earthenware dealers, from
Lane-Delf, in the Staffordshire Potteries :" whilst
behind all these, like a great yellow wall, on which
the morning sun shone dazzlingly, rose the four great
caravans of " Roarem's Menagerie," flanked, on one
hand, by the blue caravan of the Fire-Eater, and on
the other, by the red-fronted tenement of the travelling theatre. It was the beginning of a gay day—quite
a fête-day—and all looked so busy and wide awake,
that the night-capped heads were popped back again,
with the uncomfortable sense that they must have over-
slept themselves, till a glance at watch or time-piece,
or else the sweet chimes of the church clock, told them
it was only just six, and there was no reason to hurry;

The cuckoo shouted from the elm-trees, and the blackbirds sang in the pear-tree boughs; and the sun shone, and the bells began to ring; and the public-houses began to fill with farmers, clamouring for their breakfasts; and the inhabitants of the streets in which the cattle and horse-fairs were held, left their lower window-shutters closed; and jockeys began to crack off their steeds, and farmers began to handle prime stock, and the Fair was in active operation. The morning went on; the jockey's business slackened; the fat stock and the lean stock had found pur-chasers; and the more vulgar part of the business drew to an end. In the meantime, the booths and the stalls had arranged their wares. Thomas Rigley, staymaker, of Whitechapel, hung out his "corsets," in opposition to Stephen Udal, the old accredited staymaker of the town, and laughed in his sleeve at the old-fashioned cut of things which had been made out of London. James Ford, the Sheffield cutler, displayed his knives and razors in shining order; while Moses Birch, the town-cutler, assured the world around him, in a loud voice, that his wares were made to *cut*, and not, like some other folk's, only to *sell*. Morgan O'Grady exhibited horrid things in spirits, and counselled all loving parents, in his little printed papers, which flew about like leaves in autumn, to purchase for their children a pennyworth of his famous worm-gingerbread; and never since people trod upon soling leather, had been seen such tempting rows of shoes as those of Jonas Solem and the seven shoemakers of the town, who now, for the first time in their lives, agreed all together in the declaration, that if people wanted to buy shoes no better than if made of paper, they must buy them from the Stafford makers. The booths of toys were already thronged with children, who, however, as yet, speculated rather on what they should buy, than actually bought. Farmers' wives were buying cheese-colouring, and new milking-pails and butter-prints; and getting their business all done before dinner, that they and their daughters might in the afternoon have "a bit of time" for amusement. The bells rang on more merrily than ever; the streets, where the horse and cattle-fairs had been held, were now all in progress of being swept and cleaned; and now the roads and the town-ends were all thronged again with cattle going out, and country people—lads and lasses, and mothers and children, and old grandfathers and grandmothers—coming in, for the afternoon's fun and merriment. The four big men, in beef-eater costume, outside the wild-beast show, blew their trumpets, and the lion within roared from time to time; the fire-eater's performances began; and the red front of the travelling theatre had been removed, and there was now seen an open stage in front of a canvas screen, and gaily attired nymphs, who looked to vulgar eyes as if stars of gold and silver had been showered upon them, walked arm-in-arm, to and fro, attracting the admiration of village swains and big boys, who flocked thither in crowds; whilst dashing, bandit-looking men, in cloaks and plumed hats, cast half-gallant, half-ferocious glances, upon the village maidens, and thus excited in them the most charming, romantic terror, which could only be allayed by their going up, and seeing all the wonders of that enchanted world which lay behind the canvas, and of which these beings were the inhabitants.

It was now noon, and the public-houses were full

of dinners and dinner-eating guests, who did not notice, as those did who were just coming into the fair, how clouds had gathered from the south-west, and threatened rain; a gusty wind, too, had arisen, and whirled the dust along the roads, and made a strange commotion among the booths and stalls in the market-place. It grew cold and dull; and then, just when dinner was over, and everybody was in the fair, and wanted to enjoy themselves, it really began to rain, and to rain in good earnest It was no shower; there was no prospect of its soon being over; the sky was all one sullen mass of smoke-coloured cloud; and down, down, down came the soaking rain. The kennels soon ran over; and the badly-paved market-place was full of puddles, into which people unwittingly stepped, ankle-deep. It really was quite a melancholy thing to hear then the screech of a tin penny-trumpet, or the bark of a woolly dog in a little child's hand, as it stood, sheltering, with its mother, in a crowd of people, under an entry, yet never wondering, dear little soul, as they did, how in the world it was ever to get home. People had not brought umbrellas with them; and it was quite pitiable for anybody, but those who sold ribbons, to see smart girls walking along with pocket-hand-kerchiefs over their bonnets, quite wet through, and which now were all stained with the mingling and dripping dyes of their so lately blushing or verdant honours. People crowded into booths or under stalls —not to make purchases, but to find shelter; and went by throngs into the wild-beast show and the theatre, not so much to be entertained, as to get out of the rain; and all the time could think of nothing but how wet they were, and wonder how, if it kept on raining, they were ever to get home that night.

At four o'clock, at five o'clock, at six o'clock, it rained just as hard as ever, and seemed as if it would rain all night; and the public-houses were brimful: in kitchen and parlour, and bed-room, and everywhere, there was a smell of wet clothes and tobacco smoke, and ale, and gin-and-water. What was to be done? What indeed was to be done? For at that very time, there came, slowly and heavily advancing into the town, one after another, in long and weary line, seven heavy baggage wagons belonging to a regiment which had marched shortly before through the town, on its way to Ireland. Wearily went onward the wagons along the wet, grinding street, piled up, as high as the houses, with baggage, and soldiers' wives and children. The drivers were wet; the horses were wet; the soldiers who attended the train were wet; and so were the wives and children, who, wrapped in gray woollen cloaks and coats, sat up aloft among the baggage: the rain lay in large pools in the hollows of the tarpauling, and rocked about, and spilled over, as the wagons went along unsteadily up the ill-paved street; and altogether, the whole train presented a most comfortless and weary appearance. On, however, it went, wagon after wagon; and cheerful families, sitting at home by their warm firesides, were filled with a kindly compassion for the poor strangers, who had arrived thus disconsolately and thus inopportunely.

There was no room in the market-place for the unloading of the luggage; so the wagons, having made the circuit of the town, came at length to a stand in the widest part of the widest street, and began slowly to unload.

Just opposite to where they halted, stood, with its large awkward porch in front, and its large, pleasant garden behind, the little, low, old-fashioned house, inhabited by the Miss Kendricks, Joanna and Dorothy. Their parlour lay a step below the street, and its window was almost on a level with it; and, but that the pavement was always kept so nicely clean before it, must have been sadly splashed with the rain that poured down from the clouds, and dripped from, the eaves above. The Miss Kendricks were, if not among the richest, among the most respectable inhabitants of the town. Their father, in their early youth, had been the well-beloved curate of the parish—a man so pure and good, and one who so nobly and beautifully performed all his duties, great and small, that God, to reward him best, took him home to himself. His wife, heart-broken for his loss, followed him within twelve months; and left four children, Rebecca, Joanna, Leonard, and Dorothy, to the care of their great-uncle, a small shopkeeper of the place. The uncle was even then an old man—perhaps God spared his life for the sake of the orphans; and why not, when he cares even for the sparrows? He himself believed it was so; and he lived on, not only to care for the orphans, but to become of no little consequence in the place, from being for so long a time " the oldest inhabitant"—a sort of living chronicle of events; a referee on all difficult or disputed questions of right or usage. Alas! poor old man, however, all did not go on so well and smoothly as he hoped and prayed for: Rebecca, the eldest of the orphans, grew up somewhat wild and wilful, and married sorely against his will. It was a marriage of unhappiness and poverty: she and her husband removed to a remote

part of England, and vanished, as it were, entirely
from the knowledge of the family. The others, on the
contrary, grew up into the most steady and promising
manhood and womanhood. The girls he had educated
simply, as, according to his notions, might best fit
them for tradesmen's wives; but to the brother he
gave the education of a gentleman and a scholar, and
lived carefully, and almost parsimoniously himself, to
maintain him respectably at Oxford. As regarded
him, his wishes were all fulfilled; and on the evening
of the day on which the news came that Leonard had
received the degree of Bachelor of Arts, he died, as
he sat quietly in his chair. The business of his life
was done; and at the advanced age of ninety-five he
was borne to his grave, honoured by the whole town.
He left his house, and property to the amount of a
hundred a-year, to his nieces and their brother; the
house for them to live in as long as they needed such
a home, and the money to his nephew, subject to a
payment of thirty pounds a year to each sister. Miss
Joanna was seven-and-twenty at the death of her
uncle — a plain, old-fashioned little woman, who
looked six or seven years older than she was; whilst
Dorothy, on the contrary, looked younger, and though
four-and-twenty, had all the bloom and liveliness of
eighteen. Prepossessing, however, as was Dorothy,
she, at the time of her uncle's death, had no accepted
lover; whilst Joanna had been engaged to a stationer
and printer of Lichfield, of the name of Allen, for a
couple of years, and had only deferred her marriage
from reluctance to leave her old relative in the then
declining state of his health.

In such a little town as Uttoxeter, everybody knew
everybody's affairs; and therefore, no sooner was the

old gentleman dead, than all said, that for a certainty
Miss Kendrick would marry, more especially as
Leonard, who was now ordained, had the offer of a
curacy in Derbyshire, and nothing seemed more
natural than that the lively Dorothy should keep his
house. Thus the world laid out things for them;
and thus also, in the quiet of their little back parlour,
they laid out things for themselves. The great-uncle,
as we said before, was a small shopkeeper. He sold
stamps and stationery, and small cutlery ware, and
tea in sealed-up packets, as it came from the India
House: he had, altogether, a nice little ready-money
business, which amply supplied every passing week
with cash for its current expenses, and some little
besides; and it was no wonder, therefore, that after
his death, several tradesmen of the place wished to
purchase the business at a good premium.

It is an old and true saying, that " man proposes,
and God disposes;" and it was so in this case.
Leonard went to his curacy, whence he wrote the
most affectionate and charming letters, full of the
most fervent desires to do good in his parish, and to
promote the happiness of his sisters. Joanna thought
of, and made preparations for her marriage, which
was to take place as soon as the time of full mourning
for the old gentleman had expired; and in the meantime she kept on the business, prudently anxious to
spare all, and save all, against the breaking up of the
family. The weeks and months went on, and Dorothy, in the summer, paid a visit to her brother—a
golden time to her, and an earnest, as she believed it,
of the life which lay before her. It was a quiet,
out-of-the-world, Peak village, where her brother
lived; beautiful in its locality, and inhabited by people

as kind and simple-hearted as soul could wish, who received her among them as if she had been an angel from heaven; whilst the few families there, of higher rank and intelligence, seemed at once to open their hearts and homes to her.

"How well you look, Dorothy!" said Joanna to her, on her return: "the Peak air agrees with you. Your eyes look brighter, and your colour clearer than ever!"

Dorothy looked at herself in the glass, and she thought so too. Poor Dorothy! that was the last time she ever saw herself. The next day she felt unwell with headache and fever; she grew worse and worse; a medical man was called in, and in a day or two pronounced her to be ill of small-pox. We shall not go through that long and severe illness. Dorothy lay at the point of death; and her brother and sister, unable to resign her into the hands of her Maker, prayed that, at any cost, her life might be spared. Their prayers were heard. She lived; but not alone at the expense of her beauty; she lost, what was far more, her eyesight. Well, indeed, may we say, poor Dorothy! Life had now hard lessons for her—patience and submission. For herself, could she have chosen, she would rather have died than lived. She had just, as it were, become conscious of the worth of her beauty and of herself; and now she was a poor, blind ruin—a spectacle to be shunned and pitied.

"Come again to me," wrote Leonard; "the Peak air will do you good: the people here all love you, and will be kinder to you than ever."

"I will not go there, of all places in the world," said Dorothy, with bitterness; "I will not go there to be a burden to him, and a spectacle to the whole parish! Life has become hateful to me—would to God that I had died, or might die ere long!"

Joanna had the patience of an angel, and answered her sister's repinings with loving and gentle words. Winter came on; and then spring; and again the idea was revived of Dorothy's going to Leonard, for change of air; whilst Joanna, whose lover was impatient for his marriage, made her preparations for this event. But to this proposal the poor invalid would not listen. She entertained the most fixed, and as it seemed obstinate, determination not to visit her brother; nor would she assign any reason for so doing. Everybody but Joanna lost patience with her; but she, never. "She will become accustomed in time to her misfortune," said she to her friends, and, above all, to the mother and sister of her affianced lover; "and in the meantime, we must have patience with her, as with a sick child. She is now," said she, "suffering from a mind diseased, which is worse than sickness of the body. Let us only have patience with her;" and from month to month Joanna delayed her marriage, that she should not at least take so sad an invalid into the house of her husband. Day after day came his mother and sister, sometimes together, and sometimes alone, who lost no opportunity of dropping hints to poor Dorothy on the Christian duty of submission to our afflictions, and renunciation of our own wills.

"Go, and take a walk, and get a mouthful of fresh air, for you look as pale as a ghost, with all this watching and anxiety, night and day," said they continually to Joanna, in the hearing of her sister; "and we will mind the shop, and talk to Dorothy, while you are gone."

For awhile Joanna obeyed, but presently she began to perceive that the unhappy and distressful state of her sister's mind was aggravated by these interviews. Dorothy was no longer open towards her; there was a coldness and a reserve which she could not penetrate, which only increased her silence. Light, however, broke in, when the mother and sister, having, as they thought, discharged their duty to Dorothy, began to speak plainly to Joanna—she was not doing her duty either to her sister or herself, thus humouring her like a child; a degree of firmness, and even severity, was requisite. Dorothy must learn to submit; and when it pleases God to afflict us, said they, we must not stand in the way of other people's happiness with our whims and fancies. Leonard was willing to have Dorothy, and to him she ought to go; a quiet country place would furnish her with the best home: Leonard had said that he would have a girl to wait upon her; what did she want more? and then Joanna must remember that she was not using Allen well: he had had his house ready these two months, and how long did she mean to keep him waiting? If Allen had not told her himself, they would do so, that he was tired of all this waiting and waiting, and he had no notion of anything but Dorothy's going at once to her brother's, and submitting to her afflictions as any good Christian ought to do; and as Leonard, who was so good a man and preacher, would soon teach her, &c., &c., &c.!

Joanna said but little in reply, but sent over to Lichfield, to request an interview with her lover. He came; and, as plain speaking had begun, it was soon evident that he held the same opinions as his family—perhaps, indeed, that they had been employed to speak for him.　Joanna said, considering the reluctance which her sister had shown to visiting her brother, she had entirely given up the thoughts of her ever residing with him; and that, in fact, wherever her home was, there also would be Dorothy's. Allen was silent.　Joanna's spirit was roused; did he then not wish her sister to live with them?　He hummed and hawed, as people do who are ashamed of speaking out their real minds.　She then said, that he was free to choose another wife; for without she had his most full and free consent to Dorothy living with them, and to her own share of whatever the sale of the business might produce being settled upon her, she would never become his wife.

Whether Allen looked for some such consummation as this; or whether he wished it—whether he was tired of his old love, and wished to be on with a new—is not for us to say; but on hearing these words, he quietly rose up from his chair, and in a tone rather of ill-humour than grief, said, "Very well; then I suppose there will be an end of the matter."

"I suppose there will," said Joanna, without the least agitation.

"If you alter your mind before night," said he, "you can let me know; I will stay so long at my mother's."

"I shall not alter my mind," said Joanna; "and I thank God that I have found you out before it was too late."

Nothing more was said; Allen took his hat, and left the house; and Joanna did not alter her mind. The next day the mother and sister came, and were a deal more vehement on the subject than Allen had been; they upbraided her and scolded her no little, and had no mercy on the poor blind Dorothy, who, however, did not hear what was said.   It was a long, stormy day; but, like all other days, it came to an end; and Joanna, who in the course of it said that Allen had not in truth shown much *real* love for her, and could soon find another wife for his new house and furniture, was right; for, within a month of that day, he married a young lady of Lichfield; and this, his mother and sister took care to say, was the best day's work he ever did.

All this seemed easy enough for Allen; he suffered, apparently, nothing. Joanna, on the contrary, suffered much; she had loved sincerely and with her whole soul, and she threw herself now on the kind affections, and loving, though clouded heart of poor Dorothy for consolation.   Nor was she deceived. Dorothy roused herself from her lethargy, and forgot her own sorrows in alleviating those of her sister. This was the really cementing bond between them. Each bore the other's burden, and felt how good sympathy was for a wounded heart.   The reserve on the part of Dorothy gradually gave place to confidence and openness, and, in proportion as she came to speak of her morbid unhappiness, it left her.   One of her greatest trials was to allow herself to be seen; and, for this reason, she could not be induced to go out. It was quite natural, perhaps, for she had been reckoned very pretty, and had been greatly admired by all the young men of the neighbourhood; and now, though she could not see her face, she knew that she had become very plain. Great, therefore, was the good Joanna's delight, when one fine evening she said, suddenly,

" Tie that thick veil of which you have spoken on my bonnet, Joanna, and take me to Bramshall Wood.

I long to hear the gurgling of the little brook there, and to smell the cowslips : you will gather me some, and I know how they look."

Joanna could have cried for joy to hear her sister speak thus, and went with her to the wood. They sat down by the side of the little stream, the brightest and clearest of little woodland streams, and listened to the songs of the birds; and Joanna gathered flowers, which she placed in the hands of her poor blind sister.

" You have often thought me selfish and unreasonable," said Dorothy, at length ; " I know you have, and so did Mr. Allen and Martha. I know I have not been submissive," said she, preventing her sister's interruption, " and let me speak, Joanna, now, for I feel as if I could open my heart to you, and it will relieve me of a great burden; for, though I have told you many things, I have not told you all, and to-night I feel as if I could." Joanna put her arm round her sister's waist, and Dorothy continued :—

" I was very happy, formerly, very happy indeed ; I wanted nothing that I did not possess ; I had no wish beyond my own sphere, and in that sphere I possessed all that I desired, my uncle's love and yours. I was happy, too, in the consciousness of being good-looking; I felt that I had the power of pleasing; looks of admiration met me and followed me, and I was happy that it was so. Perhaps I was vain. At that time, however, I should have denied it, but now I think that perhaps I was so, and God saw right to punish me; and oh, Joanna, what a heavy punishment for so light an offence ! "

" God is good," said Joanna, with emotion, " and his chastenings are only in love ! "

"I believe it," returned Dorothy, "and I will not repine; nor is it for this that I came here to-night. I came here to ask your forgiveness for many faults, for much impatience, for much obstinacy, and perhaps in part to explain what has not been clear in me, especially as regards my unwillingness to visit Leonard. Ah, you will then see, Joanna, what reason I have to sympathise with you, for I have suffered like you! I was very happy whilst I was with Leonard: you know it; but neither he nor you know what it was that really constituted my happiness, and then made the bitterness of my misery. I loved—loved deeply and truly. Nay, do not start, Joanna—the joy and the misery are both past. I have resigned the dearest hopes of my soul at God's requiring, and the time of peace is now come!"

Dorothy was silent a few moments, and Joanna wiped away both her own tears and those which flowed from the darkened eyes of her sister.

"You have heard of Henry Ashdown, the squire's nephew. Leonard mentioned him in his letters—in the first letter, I remember, that ever he sent to us from Winston. He was a gay, but good-hearted young man, Leonard said. On the very day of my arrival at Winston, Leonard told me that Mrs. Ashdown, Henry's mother, who had been for many years a sad invalid, was then at the Hall, for her health; that, for her piety and many remarkable virtues, he had become much attached to her; and that it was his wish that I should contribute as much as possible to her comfort and amusement. I went often to see her, and thus Henry and I met. I loved the mother; but ah, I loved also the son. The mother made me the minister of her mercies to the poor, for she was the most charitable of women; and whilst Leonard read to her in pious books, I went on her errands of benevolence: but I never went alone. Leonard is simple-hearted and unsuspecting as a child, and never seemed to notice the intimacy between Henry and me. I was happy—oh, how happy!—in my love; and, though Henry never formally avowed his passion for me, his looks and actions bespoke it as plainly as words. His uncle wished him to marry the daughter of a rich neighbouring squire: his mother also acquiesced in it; for, as he was his uncle's heir, she consulted his wishes in all things. He himself, however, did not second their plans—at least, he told me so; adding, that he meant to marry to please only himself, and would give his hand where he had already given his heart. I left Winston, to return, as I fondly hoped, in a few months; and ah, how impatiently did I look forward to that time! Heaven forgive me, if in it I forgot everything. All that followed you know——Henry Ashdown never inquired after me; how was it likely that he would marry me, disfigured and blind? Oh, Almighty God, why was I spared to become the poor object that I am!"

Again Dorothy paused, and again the two sisters mingled their tears. " Yes, I know what followed," said Joanna, at length.

" Leonard's letters," continued Dorothy, "told of Henry's marriage and residence at the Hall. How could I then go to Winston?—how could I, blind though I am, sit in the same church with Henry and his bride? Oh, Joanna, what wonder then was it, when your sorrows came, that I could enter into your heart, and sympathise so deeply with you!

Hence is it that sorrow is so universal, that we may have mercy and compassion on one another!"

Joanna drew her sister yet more closely to her, and laid her head upon her bosom, and kissed her blind eyes, and felt that she had never loved her so tenderly as then.

The little shop was continued as in the time of the old uncle, and thus furnished constant occupation for Joanna; but while yet there lay upon poor Dorothy the languor of enfeebled health and of a cruelly disappointed heart, the hand of God, which chastens only in love, sent a new sorrow to bind her heart, as it were, all the more to Him. Leonard wrote thus to his sisters:—

"I am at length compelled to deal frankly with you. I am not well. I have felt very weak and poorly since the winter, when I suffered much from cold. I have latterly been much at the Hall. Mrs. Ashdown has been very kind to me, and has nursed me like a mother. I have had a physician from Ashburn, and he recommends a warmer climate. Here, even in summer, the air is keen; and as I feel myself now unable to preach, I have consented to give up the curacy for the present. I do this with the greatest reluctance, for I love the people, and I see among them a sphere of great usefulness; and if I am not able to return, I trust that God in his mercy will send hither a shepherd, who will faithfully care for his flock. At the present time, however, I yearn to be with you. My heart's desire and prayer to God is that he may make me submissive to His will. Farewell! The day after you receive this, I shall be with you."

The anxieties and sorrows of his sisters were forgotten in the distress caused by this letter. Leonard had hitherto said nothing of illness, and now they knew indeed that he must be ill to give up thus his pastoral duties. Dorothy roused herself in the sad thought of her brother's illness, and with a prophetic feeling, which she would not, however, avow to herself, that he came home to die. Blind as she was, she arranged the pillows for him on the sofa which she had hitherto occupied, with a zeal and activity of self-forgetfulness that made Joanna see the truth of her own maxim, that with every misfortune there came some compensating blessing.

Leonard returned, and even Dorothy perceived how great was the change in him : he was far gone in consumption, and the most inexperienced eye could see that he had not long to live. But that short time was as the tarriance of an angel, and left a blessing behind it. The words of love and consolation which fell from his lips were spoken in the spirit of his divine Master : " Let not your hearts be troubled ; ye believe in God, believe also in me. In my father's house are many mansions ; if it were not so, I would have told you. I go to prepare a place for you."

The influence of the dying brother was good upon both sisters, but most especially on Dorothy ; she never left her brother night nor day ; she sat with his hand in hers, like Mary at the feet of Christ, listening to his blessed words of salvation ; whilst Joanna, like Martha, though without her dissatisfied heart, waited upon them both.

Joanna feared greatly the effect which her brother's death would have on Dorothy, but the effect was different from what she expected. Whilst he lived, her very breath seemed to hang upon his ; but when his blessed spirit had departed, like David of old, she arose, and, as it were, girded herself to combat against the weaknesses of her soul, and to practise all those lessons of patience and submission, and trust in God, which she learned from him.

From this time, in the true spirit of Christian resignation, Dorothy, though blind and scarred by the ravages of a fearful disease, was never heard to complain. She discovered in herself the most remarkable sources of activity and amusement. Her hands were never idle, whilst the cheerfulness of her mind made her company really attractive. Years went on; Dorothy's once rich black hair had become white before its time; and when her sister, without explaining the cause for so doing, placed a quiet cap on her head, she submitted without remark, instinctively understanding the reason why it was done.

Joanna, when arrived at middle life, contrary to what she had done in her youth, looked younger than she really was; and, small though her income was (she had given up the shopkeeping several years before), she was really a person of some consequence in the town. In every benevolent scheme she was an operator, managing or serving; and a never-failing counsellor and comforter to the poor in difficulty or distress.

CHAPTER II.

THE OSBORNES AND THEIR FAMILY TROUBLES.

"It is a terrible evening for these poor people to arrive on," said Joanna to her sister, who sat knitting on the sofa, upon that rainy evening of May-fair day, as the baggage-wagons were unloaded before their windows, and one weary woman after another, stiff with having sat so many hours up aloft among wet boxes and tired children, was helped down from her elevation, and seemed only to put herself in motion with difficulty. The good Joanna was full of compassion, and pitied their having to find quarters in the noisy and crowded public-houses, where they would be unwelcome guests both to landlord and landlady. Greatly interested as she was by the whole arrival, her sympathies were presently enlisted on behalf of a woman who, overcome by more than fatigue, seemed unable to stand, and seated herself on one of the chests; whilst a boy, of about twelve, seemed to be the only one who took much thought about her. She was wrapped in a large gray cloak; and the hood, which was drawn over her head, partially revealed a face which was pale and dejected. The boy ran hither and thither to the various groups of women, who began to move off in various directions, and then back again, to the sick woman, for whose comfort he seemed very solicitous, for he lugged along a small chest, upon which he made her place her feet, and then wrapped her cloak about her with the most affectionate care. All this Joanna described to her sister, and then called her servant, bidding her take her pattens and umbrella, and go across, and ask if the poor woman would come in and shelter. Instead of returning with her as was expected, Joanna saw her servant give her her arm, and sheltering her with her large umbrella, move off along the street, whilst the boy trudged after, carrying a large bundle. On the return of the servant, it appeared that the woman, who was delicate, had been taken ill on the road; that she was billeted to the

2

Talbot; and, as there were two public-houses in the town of that name, it was supposed to be the one lying at some distance, whereas it proved to be the one just at hand, and thither the maid had escorted her. The woman, she said, seemed to be subdued and spiritless, as if she cared not what became of her; while the boy, on the contrary, seemed as if he would move heaven and earth to get her attended to, for he ran into the house, and demanded attention both from host and hostess, and never rested till a comfortable bed, in an upper room, was allotted to her, and then set about opening his bundle, and getting her into bed, just as if he had been a regular sick-nurse. The woman had fallen into a fainting fit, she said, just as she had told her that her mistress, Miss Kendrick, had sent her; but she thought the boy understood, as well as Mrs. Tunnicliffe, the landlady, that her mistress, who was very good to the poor, would go and see her if she was no better, and pray by her, or she could have the clergyman, if she liked it better; only he was such a young man, and many folks would much rather have Miss Kendrick than he.

Miss Kendrick was very well satisfied with what her maid had done; and commissioning her, the first thing in the morning, to run over, and inquire after the invalid, she went to bed. Scarcely, however, was the servant down-stairs the next morning, when a message came from the sick woman, requesting a little conversation with Miss Kendrick; to which was added, from the landlady, that she was so ill, she could not last long. In half an hour, Miss Kendrick was with her, and her first impression was that the hand of death was indeed upon her. She was propped up in bed, and seemed feeble in the last degree.

"Are we alone?" asked she, casting her mournful eyes round the room. "We are, mother," said the boy, throwing himself on his knees at the bed's foot; "there is only the lady, and you and me."

She looked steadily at Miss Kendrick, and then said, slowly and with difficulty, "I am Rebecca—your unhappy, outcast sister. God brought me here to die. I knew it as I entered the town, when the baggage-train could not enter the market-place, but made halt before the very house where I had been a child—from whence I set out when I took my fate into my own hands!"

Joanna, petrified with astonishment and compassion, seized her hand and gazed into her face.

"Yes," said the woman, "I am Rebecca, your sister, though you may not recognise me."

"My poor, unhappy sister!" exclaimed Joanna, embracing her with tears. "Thank God that you are found at last! You shall live with us—with Dorothy and me—you shall yet be happy!"

"Never more in this world!" interrupted she. "I know I have not long to live, and yet I have much to say—let me speak while I have the power.—My first husband died. I thought to mend my condition. I married a second time; but there was not a blessing on anything I did. I married yet more unhappily. I have had nine children by my two husbands. The youngest child, a girl, is left behind with its grandmother,—a good woman. This is my youngest boy,—he is my Benjamin. The two older than he died. It was good for them. Of the other six two are married, two are beyond seas, and one—oh my God, have pity on the outcasts of society; for all are thy children!" After a long pause, she again pro-

ceeded :—"My husband is a soldier,—a private in the
———, now in Ireland, and which we follow. He was
a very handsome man ; and that was my bane. He
was of an unbroken temper, and was not loved in the
regiment. I suffered much from him; and yet I
would not leave him. I always went with the regiment; for the officers' ladies liked me. I was a good
laundress, and got up their fine linens to their mind ;
and for this reason, spite of my poor health, was permitted to accompany the regiment to Ireland. I was,
however, taken very ill on the journey. I began to
spit blood ; and at Wolverhampton, I felt it was all
over with me ; for a dreadful thing came to my
knowledge there."   With these words she drew
from under her pillow a part of a newspaper,
which she put into Joanna's hand, and bade her
read, but not aloud.   She read how one Peter
Reynolds, a private in the ——— regiment of foot
soldiers, bound for Ireland, who had been guilty
of some misdemeanor on the march, had deserted immediately on their arrival in Dublin,
been retaken, and sentenced by court-martial to be
shot.

   "He is my husband," said the poor dying woman
after a time. "I thought I should have died as I
read the paper. I told nobody, however, but him,"
said she, looking at the boy, "and he has the sense
of a grown man. I knew how little Reynolds was
liked in the regiment, and that there was no hope
for him ; and for that reason I wanted all the more
to see him before it happened. I thought I might comfort him ; for oh, it's a dreadful thing to die in that
way, when a man's in his full strength." She could
say no more. Her distress of mind was excessive ;

and one fainting fit succeeded another so rapidly that she was unable to converse again through the day. The boy in the meantime, who showed the strongest affection towards her, and an intelligence and prudence beyond his years, won the entire love of Joanna.

In the evening, as the sick woman seemed somewhat better, she was removed on a bed to the house of her sisters; and in three days from that time she died. It was an event of course which made a deal of talk in the town. Many people remembered Rebecca Kendrick and her unhappy marriage; but to the great joy of her sisters, the miserable and disgraceful end of her second husband was never or scarcely known in the town.

"I wonder whether Mr. Osborne would take poor William as an apprentice," said Dorothy to her sister a day or two after the funeral; "a chemist and druggist's is a good business, and they are such kind people."

"I have thought of that too," returned Joanna, "for we will do all we can for him; what a clever, nice boy he is! But it is odd that we have seen nothing of the Osbornes for these three or four days; nor have they sent down to inquire after us. However, when it gets dusk, I will put on my things and go and have some talk with them about William."

The Osbornes were Miss Kendrick's most intimate friends. He, as it may be inferred, was a chemist and druggist. He had one of those dingy, oldfashioned shops, saturated with the smell of drugs and physic, which are only to be found in oldfashioned places. His wife and he, who had no family, were patterns of conjugal felicity; each thinking the other as near perfection as poor human nature could be; and they were not very far from the mark, for better people than they, making allowance for some little intermixture of human weakness, could hardly be found. They had been fast, life-long friends of the Kendricks; and not a week passed without their spending an evening together It was no wonder, therefore, that Joanna was surprised that for the last three or four days they had heard nothing of them. Joanna resolved to go to them when it was dusk; but as it is not yet dusk, we shall find the interval very convenient for making the reader acquainted with some farther particulars regarding them, which it is very important for him to know.

Mr. and Mrs. Osborne were now somewhat past middle life, and had been married nearly thirty years. At the time of her marriage, there was a young sister, the daughter of her father by a second marriage, dependent upon her. The mother died in giving birth to this child, who, however, never felt her loss in the love and care of her elder sister. The father died when she was about ten years old; and soon afterwards the elder sister married; and in her husband the child found a second father. She grew up gentle and beautiful; and the love of this affectionate pair was lavished upon her. Never was girl more tenderly nurtured, more beloved, or more indulged. She had all her heart could wish; and she appeared to deserve it.

The Osbornes, though tradespeople, were well to do, and the young lady was admitted to the best society of the place; and as she advanced towards womanhood, had the chance of making several advantageous matches. For some time she appeared difficult to please, till at length a gay young stranger, whom she accidentally met with, fixed her fancy. Her friends objected somewhat to the match. In the first place, he was a stranger; in the second place, he lived far off, that is to say, in Liverpool; and to them, who wished to have their darling fixed near to them for life, Liverpool seemed a long way off; thirdly, and which was most important of all, there was a something—an indescribable something— about this Louis Edwards which was unsatisfactory to the plain-dealing and straightforward sincerity of Mr. Osborne. He was plausible, had a reason for everything, and though he was an American by birth and connections, he had lived so many years in England as to be English in his feelings. Still for all that, and though he was a broker by trade, and had a partner, a man of reputation and substance, and had altogether a very imposing manner, Mr. Osborne never liked him; and felt so strongly that there *was* a something, though it was impossible to say what, which created misgivings, that he and his wife refused their consent.

Edwards was dismissed; and the loving, gentle, all-acquiescent Phebe promised to give him up. If there be an occasion beyond all others which awakens the affection of parents to their children—and the Osbornes were as parents to Phebe—it is when they see a child submissively giving up its beloved will and wishes to their sterner reason and judgment. The Osbornes felt thus, and thought that they could not sufficiently show their affection to her; and were devising a thousand little schemes for her happiness and indulgence, when one dreary day in November she was gone! They could not conceive whither, till the second day's post brought a letter from her beseeching their forgiveness, and saying that as she knew they desired her happiness, they must allow her to become happy in her own way, which was by uniting her fate to that of Edwards. This she had done, and must now throw herself on their mercy, assuring them that her future life should prove how grateful she was for all their former kindness.

A letter like this is at such a time a mockery. Better by far is it to weep over a child borne to the grave with all its young fair promise in the bud, than to see one that we love as our own life running wilfully and headlong into ruin spite of all our warning and our prayers! The Osbornes thought so. Her deceit and disobedience cut them to the heart, and their prejudices were only the more strengthened against a match which had begun so badly. Grieved however as they were, from the bottom of their souls they pitied her; for they felt sure that a time would come when she would bitterly repent.

"Alas, Phebe," said good Mr. Osborne in his reply to her letter, "what is this which you have done! But we will not speak of the sorrow which we foresee. May God bless you, though you have grieved us sorely! You are young, and life lies all before you; be a good wife; be true to your husband in good and in evil; atone for your want of duty to us by your duty to him; and so may God Almighty bless you!"

The Osbornes did not turn their backs on Phebe; but remembered her in sorrow rather than in anger; and this strong proof of their affection touched her much more deeply than any evidences of their displeasure could have done. The match, however, in a worldly point of view, did not appear so bad.

Edwards lived handsomely; and, though Phebe could never persuade her brother and sister to visit her, she failed not to tell them of her prosperity, of her gay life and acquaintance, and of her happiness as a wife and mother. Whether, however, she gave a brighter colouring to things than they deserved; whether she wished to deceive others, or was herself deceived, we cannot say; but at the very time when she was writing of her happiness and prosperity, her husband's name appeared in the gazette, and they were deeply insolvent bankrupts.

"The world is not surprised, my dear Phebe, at what has happened, however you may be," wrote Mr. Osborne to her, "nor are we. The time of trial is now come; faint not now, nor lose courage; and above all things do not forget God, who chastises us only in love."

Poor Phebe! the time of trial was indeed come; and, for the first time in her life, she learnt what it was to deny herself and take up her cross daily. Every one finds this to be a hard lesson; and Phebe was one to feel it bitterly. Edwards removed from Liverpool to London; had one clerkship after another, and lived as he could, now with money and now without; yet never losing his unabashed plausibility, and buoying himself up with the notion that after all he should do somehow or other.

Few and far between were the letters which Phebe wrote to her friends; and though she never complained of narrow circumstances, she wrote mournfully of the sickness and death of two of her children. The Osbornes on their part were extremely anxious about her; and though she never solicited aid from them, the five and ten-pound notes which good Mr. Osborne occasionally inclosed were always thankfully accepted. They invited her and her one remaining child to come and visit them,—to remain through a long winter with them; but this she declined, without assigning any reason for so doing.

Not long afterwards, however, she wrote to them a humble letter, and one which bore evidence of being written with difficulty; it was on behalf of her husband, to beg the loan of a few hundred pounds, as he had the chance of entering into partnership in a speculation which promised to return cent. per cent. Mr. Osborne refused, on the plea of want of confidence in Edwards and his schemes. The next post brought a letter from Edwards himself, full of the most plausible statements regarding his scheme, and urging the loan of the money almost as a right on behalf of his wife. This letter was immediately followed by one from Phebe to her sister, begging her in the most urgent and moving terms to use her influence with her husband, as not only Edwards' worldly prosperity depended on this money being raised, but her own happiness also. There was an urgent tone of almost desperation in the letter, and an instability in the handwriting, that showed the most agitated state of mind. The Osbornes were moved; and, accompanying the money with a letter of grave tradesman-like advice to Edwards, Mr. Osborne remitted it on no other security than his note.

Within a few months, Phebe wrote again; the cloud had evidently passed away; but from this time the tone of her letters was much more serious than formerly. She spoke little of her husband, but much of her child, then six years old, of which she seemed extremely fond. A year went on, and letters came but seldom; a second year, and then Edwards and his partner were again bankrupt. Edwards accused his partner of roguery and mismanagement, and some person who accidentally had seen Phebe in London brought news of her wan and care-worn appearance.

The relations thought more of her distress than of the loss of their money. For two more years nothing was heard of them ; and how they lived never came to their relations' knowledge. At length, one winter's day, a woman wrapped in a large plaid cloak knocked at the private door and begged to speak with Mrs. Osborne alone. After some hesitation she was brought in ; and when they two were together, she announced herself as Phebe Edwards.

"I know how shocked you are to see me," said she, "I am greatly changed; but that is of small account. I am become regardless of my looks."

The good people wept over her ; and received her as the father in the gospel received his prodigal son.

"You are come to stay with us," said they, "you will never leave us again."

"I am going again to-night," said Phebe, "my business is urgent. I dared not write, nor would I let Edwards come himself."

She then explained that by the kind interference of a gentleman who had known her husband in Liverpool, he had the chance of a situation in a banking-house in London, provided some responsible man would be surety for him to the amount of five hundred pounds. Phebe paused ; for the money her brother-in-law had already lost by her husband was in her mind, and she saw that it was in his also.

"I know your thoughts," said she, "and because you have already suffered so much, I would not write to you ; but, brother, it is the privilege of the good to forgive injuries—to return good for evil. Forgive us, therefore, what you have already suffered from us; I have prayed God to forgive us, even as I know you had done, and you will not close your heart against us. Oh!" said she, clasping together her hands, and fixing upon him her large, sunken, and tearless eyes, "I have made my child pray to God every night to bless you; because I thought that the prayers of a child most surely ascended to heaven! I know," continued she more calmly, "that you have very little reason to trust either Edwards or me; but if you cast us off, then are we lost for ever! I do not pretend or attempt to excuse Edwards; but he is heartily sorry for the past—he has been unfortunate, we have all suffered much, and we are all humble now; and from you we ask this one chance of regaining our place in society!"

"Oh stay with us, Phebe," said Mrs. Osborne, quite overcome by her sister's words, "stay with us, and you and your child shall never want."

"The first letter," returned Phebe, "which I received from Mr. Osborne after my marriage, contained these words, 'atone for your want of duty to us by your duty to your husband, and so may God Almighty bless you!' these words I have never forgotten. They have been hitherto, and shall still be, the law of my life; let my husband's fortune be what it may, I abide with him to the last."

"She is right, Sarah, she is right," said Mr. Osborne, wiping his eyes and rising from his seat; "and I will be surety for Edwards for her sake. I will give him this one trial more."

Poor Phebe, who hitherto had not shed one tear,

now overcome by the generous kindness of her brother, covered her face with both her hands and wept like a child. How the rest of the day was spent may easily be imagined; the best which the house could offer was set before her; and her sister, taking her into her own chamber, questioned her closely of her wants and actual condition. But whatever Phebe's sufferings had been, she kept much to herself. To poverty she confessed, and to all the hardships and anxieties which poverty brings with it; but not one word did she utter against her husband, although her sister never lost the impression that she had suffered much unkindness from him.

True to her first intentions, she returned by coach that night to London, taking with her good store of many things which the bounty and overflowing affection of her sister heaped upon her.

Phebe's visit had entirely reinstated her in the hearts of her relations, and the next year Mr. Osborne did such an unheard-of thing as go to London himself, on business he said, but in reality to see her and her children: for a second child, a little girl, was now born to her. On his return, he related that they were living quietly, and with some appearance of comfort; but that there was still a look of depression and anxiety about her, while Edwards on the contrary seemed scarcely changed, excepting that he was grown slightly grey and much stouter than when he married; but he was as well dressed as then; as gay in spirits, as plausible; and to the conscientious and somewhat suspicious mind of Mr. Osborne, as unsatisfactory as ever. For his own peace of mind as regarded them, it was a pity that he had ever been to visit them. The only thing that gave them real

3

satisfaction was that Edwards retained his situation; and at the end of the second year received an increase of salary, which Phebe did not fail to communicate to her relations. Three years had now gone on, and we are arrived at the period when our story opens.

The Osbornes and the Kendricks were, as we have said, fast friends; the somewhat similar marriages of Phebe and the unhappy Rebecca, had made, for years, a great sympathy of feeling between them. Mrs. Osborne was at their house, and sitting by the side of Rebecca's bed when she died, and her husband had attended her to the grave.

Much attached, however, as they were to their friends, they said nothing of the disgrace which had befallen Rebecca's husband and the father of the nephew whom they had adopted, thinking, with a natural and jealous feeling of family pride, that there was no good in publishing the dishonour of one's own connexions.

Some such feeling as this operated on the mind of good Mrs. Osborne as she sat in the dusk of evening in the little parlour beside the shop, with the candles unlighted, and heard her friend Miss Kendrick inquire with astonishment about Mr. Osborne's sudden journey to London, of which Mr. Isaacs the shopman had told her.

Yes, said Mrs. Osborne, but in an incommunicative tone, her husband was suddenly called to London by a letter from poor Phebe. She feared things were going on but badly with them,—how, she did not say, merely adding, "but I wish nothing to be said about it; the least said the better as we all know."

Joanna was a reasonable woman, and she excused

her friend's reserve, sincerely sympathising with her in having any new cause of anxiety and distress. Leaving her, therefore, to open her business respecting her nephew to Mrs. Osborne as a sort of preliminary step in the affair, we will communicate to the reader that unhappy circumstance regarding the Edwards's, which Joanna knew only later.

The letter which Phebe had written was rather indefinite, but one which filled those to whom it was addressed with horror. It spoke of temptation and crime, of loss of character for ever, and of the severest punishment of the law, and besought her brother-in-law to hasten to them immediately. He did so, and found his worst fears to be true. Edwards had been again tempted to embark in some wild speculation; money was wanted which his own means did not supply, and having gained the confidence of his employers, he had taken advantage of it, and had, at two several times, drawn money from the bank by forged orders in the names of merchants who had large dealings with the house. In the first instance, six months had elapsed without detection; in the second, to a larger amount, detection came speedily.

On the first moment of alarm, he had escaped on board a vessel bound for Hamburgh; but had been pursued and taken while the vessel was under weigh. There was not a word to be said in his extenuation; the fact was as it were proved upon him; he was in the fangs of the law, and was committed to take his trial.

Such were the facts respecting which Mrs. Osborne might well be excused from saying much. In a week's time her husband was again at home; and Miss Kendrick made application on behalf of her

nephew being apprenticed to his business. Mr. Osborne said that he had just engaged a young apprentice, whom he shortly expected; that two at once
was rather too much; but considering the case of
poor Reynolds, and that it was to oblige Miss Kendrick, he would talk with Mr. Isaacs and see if it
could not be arranged; and that she should know in
a day or two. Within a day or two, Joanna and her
sister resolved upon going to Matlock for a few weeks,
and taking their nephew with them; so that there
was full time to deliberate. The season was fine.
Miss Kendrick found company to their taste at
Matlock; and to the great joy of the boy, who now
for the first time in his life knew what ease and
pleasure were, the stay was lengthened to the end of
July.

On their return, Miss Kendrick went to hear the
decision of her friend the druggist; again he was not
in the shop, but there stood behind the counter a
slim, gentlemanly youth, who, under the direction of
Mr. Isaacs, was folding up, very successfully, penny-
worths of Epsom salts and flowers of brimstone. This
was evidently the new apprentice of whom Mr. Osborne had spoken. On inquiring for that gentleman,
Miss Kendrick learned, to her surprise, that both he
and his wife were in London.

" It must be about that miserable business of the
Edwards's," said she to Dorothy on her return. Of
course it was, and all the town knew it by this time;
for the newspapers had detailed the affair from one
end of the kingdom to the other.

The trial was now over. Edwards had pleaded
his own cause most skilfully and eloquently, but in
vain; he was found guilty, and condemned to four-

teen years' transportation. On hearing his sentence, Edwards seemed to feel, for the first time, the crushing weight of his unhappy circumstances. A paleness as of death overspread his countenance ; and, but for the support of the turnkey, he would have fallen to the ground. Mr. Osborne visited him the next day in prison; and, for the first time in his life, felt compassion for him. Edwards was in fact a man of real talent and great power of mind, with some tendencies to good ; but alas ! he was one of those who have not the ability to resist temptation. He was of a sanguine temperament, and was always confident of success. When, therefore, humiliation' and failure *did* come, he was only the more cast down. His spirit was now broken, and the better parts of his character came forth. These, as it were, took the kind heart of Mr. Osborne by surprise ; and now, with a reaction of feeling which is very natural to a generous mind, he felt as if he must compensate for his hitherto hard judgment; and this he did by more than free forgiveness.

Phebe during the whole time had been calm and collected. The worst had come that could come ; and God and good men had not abandoned her. That kind brother, who had been as a father to her in her youth, stood by her in this hour of trial. He had already adopted her son as his own; and thus removed, as it were, from the knowledge and contamination of evil, she trusted that his course through life might be easier and happier than that of his parents. Phebe's resolve from the first had been to remove with her youngest child, a little girl of two years old, to the land where her husband was now a banished man. Her brother made no objection; and

he and his wife accordingly came up, two weeks before the time of her departure, to provide for her
comforts on the voyage, and to take leave of her for
ever. She sailed at the beginning of August; and
the convict ship in which was her husband at the end
of the same month.

Their careers seemed thus brought to an end in
this hemisphere; and therefore leaving them, the one
with his weaknesses and his misdeeds, the other expi-
ating the errors of her youth by a life of patience and
duty, we will turn more particularly to the son, who
will henceforth be one of the principal heroes of our
little story.

CHAPTER III.

THE TWO APPRENTICES.

THE youth, like his father, was called Louis, with
the additional Christian name of William, which his
mother had given to him in love and grateful remem-
brance of her brother-in-law Mr. Osborne; and now
his good uncle and aunt, anxious to remove from him
any infamy connected with his father's misconduct,
transposed and slightly altered his names, and called
him Edward Lewis Williams.   Edward Williams
was therefore only an ordinary young apprentice—it
was given out that he was an orphan—with whose
history the world had nothing to do; and though
Mr. Isaacs and the whole household soon saw that he
was not treated like an ordinary apprentice, the world
did not readily conjecture that he was the son of the
convict Edwards.

"Let Williams come into the parlour," said Mr.

Osborne, as he was leaving the shop for the evening, to his assistant Mr. Isaacs, "I would have a little talk with him before his fellow-apprentice comes; he seems a sharp, clever youth, I think," said Mr. Osborne.

"A little too much of a gentleman at present," returned Mr. Isaacs, who was a thorough tradesman, and had no patience with any dandyism behind the counter, "and sharp and clever he is with a witness; he has broken half a gross of vials, two graduated measures, and a Corbyn quart, within the last fortnight; but he has taken prodigiously to practical chemistry, and so that he does not blow the house up, he may be of some use in time."

"We must teach him to be careful," said Mr. Osborne, advancing to the door, "send him in as soon as he comes," repeated he, and disappeared through the half-glass door with the green silk curtain, that led to the parlour where his good wife always sat at her work.

Mr. Osborne had a little code of morals—it is a thousand pities that it never was printed—which he delivered orally to his apprentices many times during the earlier part of their apprenticeship; and he now wished particularly to insist on that part which re-lated to "your duties towards your fellow-apprentices." This warned of bad example, either set by themselves or followed in others; insisted on truth, sobriety, kindness; on advising in love; on "doing as they would be done by." Mrs. Osborne always cried when her husband thus lectured his young apprentices. She felt as if the boys were her own children, and she always said that no clergyman could preach to them as her husband did. "And now remember," concluded Mr. Osborne, "that the happiness and well-being of your future life depend upon the dispositions you cultivate and the habits you acquire in youth ;—are you idle, wasteful, unpunctual, dilatory in youth, it is vain to look for industry, frugality, exactness, and promptitude in after-life. *A religious, active youth will ensure, as far as human means can do it, a respectable and prosperous age!*" These last words Mr. Osborne never failed to speak with remarkable emphasis, nor did he omit it on this occasion. Thus far, the young apprentice had been fed with what may be called, in the style of Jean Paul or our Carlyle, the common apprentice-bread; afterwards came the cake-of-love which was broken for his especial eating; and this was literally a love-feast, at which the good aunt as well as uncle assisted.

Some little they said on his peculiar circumstances, on the awful example which would ever remain before him in his father's career; but oh, how tenderly and lovingly was this warning enforced! The youth —and he was a slender, handsome youth—sat with his graceful head supported on his well-formed hand, and his intelligent brown eyes fixed on the countenance of his affectionate monitors. He looked handsome; and they saw in him the fairest promises of good,—they saw in him the support, and comfort, and pride of their old age. They besought him to be steadfast in his duties both to God and man; they besought him to deserve the love which they were willing to give him; and in them, they said, he should never want a friend. They spoke with tears, and as the seal of the covenant between them, they gave him a new Bible, which they prayed him to study diligently. The youth began to say something about gratitude; but his voice trembled, and he was so much affected that he could not go on. The old people gave him their hands, and said that it was not needful; they understood his feelings, and were sure he would try to deserve their love.

Mrs. Osborne ordered in a very good supper that night; the apple-pie that had been intended for the morrow's dinner was sent in, and cold beef, and pickle, and roast potatoes with plenty of butter; and then the smart young apprentice went out to put up the shop-shutters, secretly rejoicing to himself that it was for the last time, inasmuch as the new apprentice would come the next day, and then, as the junior, this would henceforth be his duty.

We have spoken of the Osbornes' love-feast; the Miss Kendricks also made one for their nephew, which they intended should last for a whole day. They hired a post-chaise, and drove to the pleasant village of Hanbury in Needwood Forest, where lived some old friends of theirs,—a good farmer and his wife. Their nephew walked about the farmer's abundant garden, and ate fresh-gathered apples from the trees, and strolled out by himself into the fields, and came home just in time for dinner. And what a dinner it was, with game, and hot apple-pie, and cream, and syllabubs! and how merry the little fat farmer was, and his wife too, and how they all ate, and drank, and chatted, and laughed! Even Aunt Dorothy, she was as merry as anybody.

After dinner, William went out again by himself. He had been rather low-spirited the day before about leaving the aunts that he loved so well and going 'prentice; but now all dull thoughts seemed driven away. There was something inspiriting in the bright, breezy autumn air, as he strolled along through the old pasture fields, and saw the feathery seeds of the thistle and the great groundsel lifted up and carried over his head by the wind, and the yellow harvest-fields lying amid the deep repose of the woodlands around, and the harvesters piling up the golden shocks of corn on the heavy wain, which moved on-ward now and then, silently as in a dream. He sat down on the dry slope of the field, with the little shrubby tufts of the rosy-hued rest-harrow at his feet; and thought about his past life and his future. There was a deal of hardship, and sorrow, and trouble in his past life, which was best known to himself and to his Almighty Father; and which he someway or other shrunk from telling to his kind aunts. There was no use in telling it to them, he thought, and he was right; for it would have done them no good, nor him either. All this now passed in clear review be-fore him; it was like a procession of dark shadows; one after another they went by, and ended in that wet night of May-fair day and his mother's death. But yet that death was not as sad as many things in her life had been; and the boy thought of her grave in the little churchyard of her native town as of her truest resting-place. The only pleasant thought in the past was of his little sister,—the little rosy-cheeked Susan, who was left with the old Methodist grandmother at Truro in Cornwall. Susan was very happy; and above all things liked going with the old woman to chapel, where the people all sang so loud. It was a pleasant thought, that of Susan. Then came his aunts,—Dorothy, blind, and with her hair like snow, yet as cheerful as a lark, and so active! No-body that saw her at home could ever think her

blind! And Joanna, who never thought about herself, but was always working or scheming for the
good of somebody or other; who was full of resources
for every difficulty, and who suggested good motives
for everybody's actions. Never in all this world,
poor William thought, were there better women
than his aunts; it would be impossible for him to
turn out badly, belonging, as he did, to such good
people. William thought of all the pleasure they
had given him, of the happy weeks at Matlock, of
the collection of minerals they had bought for him,
of the new clothes they had given him,—how they
were about to put him apprentice to a respectable
business, how they had given him a new Bible and
such a handsome prayer-book as would make it a
pleasure to go to church; and to wind up all, how
they had hired a chaise and brought him out into the
country, which he enjoyed so much, just on purpose
to make his last day of freedom pleasant. All this he
thought of, and then made a little vow with himself
that he would be very obedient and good as an apprentice, and be industrious in learning his business;
and then, when he was a man and his aunts were
old, that he might be able to do something for them
in return. He grew quite in love with his good
resolves, and then fell into a charming day-dream of
happily-accomplished wishes, from which he was
roused by the sound of voices and the creaking of
a loaded wagon, which, with its piled-up sheaves,
went brushing slowly past the tall hedge-row trees
behind him. It was the wagon which, two hours
before, he had been watching in the distant fields;
and then the thought first occurred to him that it
was time for him to go back to the farm-house. He

ran hastily back, buoyant-hearted with all his good resolutions, and was a little alarmed to see the post-chaise standing at the door. Aunt Dorothy and the farmer's wife were seated on the horse-block, and Joanna and the farmer were looking out from the farm-yard gate; they evidently were looking for him, and then, all at once, for the first time since he had been out, he remembered that his aunt Joanna had warned him not to be long, not above an hour; for they wanted to be at home in good time—how could he have forgotten? Aunt Joanna looked displeased as he came up; he had never seen her look displeased before.

"Well, youngster, we've had a pretty hunt for you," said the farmer, when he reached the gate.

"You must have forgotten what I said," remarked Aunt Joanna.

"Ah, Master William," began the farmer's wife, "I've had a pretty time to pacify your Aunt Dorothy; she thought you must have got drowned, or some mischief."

"I am very sorry," said William; and felt quite humble and submissive, but there was no time or opportunity to say more. He hurried into the parlour to have tea, or coffee, or wine. There was plum-cake, seed-cake, and bread and butter: he must have something—he could eat nothing; he wanted so much to make his peace with everybody. But there was no chance for his getting in a word; his aunts, and the farmer and his wife, were at the chaise-door, in the full energy and activity of leave-taking. There was a basket full of eggs, a bottle of cream, and some fresh butter to go into the chaise; there was a hamper of apples and a couple of fowls to be stowed away, for all of which the aunts had, first of all, to express astonishment, and then thanks; and, amid all this, they and their nephew seated themselves in the chaise, and off they drove. William sat silent, and felt unhappy; his heart trembled at the thought of anger; he had seen so much of it formerly, and so little of it in the last happy weeks of his life. He wished his aunts would but begin to talk; but for some time they did not, nor did he.

At length began Aunt Joanna:—" My dear boy," said she, " nothing will be more necessary to you, in life, than strict punctuality. Now, when I had told you to be back soon, what could keep you out so long—when you might see that it was getting late, and the dew was falling. What were you doing ?"

" Nothing," said he.

" Nothing !" she repeated. " That is hardly likely—an active boy like you must have been doing something."

William might have said that he had been busy with his thoughts, reviewing the past, and making good resolves for the future. He thought of saying so; but then it occurred to him that perhaps his aunts would not believe him: he had often been disbelieved in former days, when he had spoken the honest truth. A sullen cloud, like the spirit of those dark former days, fell upon him, and he again replied to his aunt's question, three times repeated, that " he had been doing nothing."

His aunt said no more. Neither she nor Dorothy said much during the rest of the drive homeward; they were sorry to see him, as they thought, per-

verse and sullen, and not wishing to excite an
antagonist spirit, which they fancied they saw in
him, they sat silent, and mourned to themselves.

He, on his part, sat between them, dispirited and
out of humour. This was the end, then, of all his
good resolutions: nobody would give him credit for
meaning to do right—that was always the way.
His aunts, after all, were as unjust as anybody else.
All his good resolutions seemed folly and nonsense;
he despised himself for them, and said, in his own
heart, that it was no use trying to be good. The
dark phantoms which he had called up from the
past, and made to pass before him, seemed to have
possession of him, and he remembered mournfully
the chapter which, the evening before, he had read
in his new Bible to his Aunt Dorothy, of him who
took seven other spirits unto him worse than himself, and the last state of that man was worse than
the first.

So ended *their* Love Feast. But it was a real
Love Feast for all that. It was only as if the love-
cake had been a little burned in the baking—human
endeavours are so seldom perfect.

But now, for six months after this time. Mr.
Isaacs went to church every Sunday evening; and,
as the Osbornes' pew adjoined that of the Miss
Kendricks, and they regularly attended church
twice in the day, which Mrs. Osborne did not,
because her husband only went in the morning, he
mostly walked home with them; and when there
was no moon, and the streets therefore as good as
dark—for the scanty oil lamps were not worth
speaking of—he offered an arm to each sister, which
had given rise, in the minds of the two most noto-

rious gossips of the place, Mrs. Morley and Mrs. Proctor, that Mr. Isaacs had a liking for Miss Joanna Kendrick. The report had even reached the ears of the parties themselves; but they seemed so amazingly indifferent about it, that people left them to do as they would, only just speaking of it now and then to keep the idea alive, as a town corporation walks its parish boundaries every seven years or so, to keep their memory from dying out.

"And how does William get on," asked Miss Kendrick, therefore, one Sunday evening, from Mr. Isaacs, on whose arm she leaned.

"Pretty well," said he, in a half-hesitating tone.

"Only pretty well, still!" she returned.

"Why, you see," said Isaacs, "he has not the natural facility of mind that Williams has. That youth has something quite uncommon about him—if he had but stability he might do anything. They now take regular Latin lessons, and that prevents his attending to many other things. Latin is absolutely necessary, and they neither of them understood a word of it."

"What, then," began Joanna, somewhat cheered, "had this clever youth been as much neglected as our poor nephew?"

"He has knowledge enough, and to spare," said Isaacs, "but not exactly of the right kind; he is prodigiously smart and clever, and knows how to make the most of what he has. If he have but stability and good conduct, he may get on wonderfully."

These words sunk deep into the hearts of both aunts. How was it? Was Williams above the average capacity of youths, or was their nephew below it? They were troubled and discontented. They feared that he did not make all the efforts in his power; perhaps he was careless and inattentive : they must talk with him, and try to rouse up a spirit of emulation in him. Next moment, they were half-disposed to be out of humour with his companion's facility of mind—it is so unpleasant to be outstripped ourselves, or to see those one loves and cares for outstripped.

The next evening, the aunts sent their compliments to Mr. Osborne, and begged that he would let their nephew drink tea with them. He came, and by the gentlest manœuvres in the world, the affectionate aunts began to test the young apprentice's knowledge and skill. How did he like his business?—did he feel that he was getting on at all?—did light begin to break in upon him in any way?—did he feel that he could keep up with Williams? To these questions he replied, that he *did* like his business—that he felt he was getting on—light was breaking in upon him, even in Latin ; he had made up a prescription that very day—but as to keeping up with Williams, that was not an easy thing. Williams could make out a prescription above a month ago. Williams was so very clever, he could do anything that he liked ; he learned without the least trouble, and had such a memory as never was !

Such was his report of his fellow-apprentice. The aunts listened in silence, and concluded that it must be as Mr. Isaacs had said ; Williams was a youth of extraordinary abilities. They sighed over their nephew, who seemed to have but common abilities, and were kinder to him than ever ; perhaps to compensate, if they could, for Nature's supposed unkindness. But long was the lecture that they gave to him on patience and perseverance, which, plodding on together, remove mountains of all kinds, and make even ordinary abilities more availing than the most meteor-like genius.

"Well, and how does Reynolds go on?" again inquired Joanna from Mr. Isaacs, some twelve or eighteen months later.

"Exceedingly well!" was now the reply. "He has stability and perseverance, he will make a good tradesman. He is much more practical than Williams, and thus much more useful." The aunts were well pleased, and now could very well endure to hear their nephew speak well of his fellow-apprentice.

The Osbornes, who had their reasons for being particularly interested in Williams, saw his quick abilities, and his attractive exterior, with uncommon pleasure. As to Mr. Isaacs, he had begun some time ago to have his own thoughts about the smart apprentice, and let him now take his own flights, satisfied to have the more helpful services of Reynolds. Isaacs soon saw, what Mr. Osborne seemed never to find out, that Williams, unstable as water, 'spite of his natural brilliant gifts, would, in the end, excel in nothing. Besides this, there were slight peccadilloes now and then, a missing half-crown or so, which, while he never shut his own eyes to, and always reproved in his own way, he never spoke of to Mr. or Mrs. Osborne, unwilling to distress them, as he said to himself, about the son of poor Mrs. Edwards.

Mr. Isaacs had mentioned to Miss Kendricks his suspicion of the youth's parentage; and this suspicion was confirmed to them by an accidental discovery which their nephew made of what seemed to him the transposed name of his companion, written in his Prayer-book, "William Louis Edwards;" and which, on being shown to him, he immediately tore from the book, saying gaily that it was only a joke. But Williams's secret was safe, both with Miss Kendricks and Mr. Isaacs; and, while the youth did not trouble himself one jot about either the one or the other, he grew tall and good-looking, and, though he wore a shop-apron, had not at all the look of a tradesman about him.

Time went on: the fellow-apprentices agreed remarkably well together. Reynolds plodded on at the quiet drudgery of his business, and Williams took discursive flights of all kinds. Now he was deep among gases, and now he was up in the clouds among the fascinations of the circulating library; now he dipped here and there into the Materia Medica and Dr. Thomas's Practice of Physic; and now he laboured for three months in learning to play the flute. He certainly had a variety of tastes, if not of talents; and the Osbornes, good people as they were, saw this as something quite remarkable. Mrs. Osborne was fascinated with his handsome figure and gentlemanly bearing, with his amusing conversation, and his variety of little social talents and accomplishments. She contrasted him, in her own mind, with the more homely, unassuming Reynolds. "Poor Miss Kendricks," thought she, "how proud they would be to have a nephew like ours!"

She was the kindest-hearted woman that ever lived; and she never thought thus without being touched with compassion for the good, humbly-gifted youth, as she thought Reynolds; and many a little kindness and indulgence did he unwittingly owe to this sentiment in her heart towards him.

Time went on, and yet on. The apprentices had each gone on in their own way, and were both nearly nineteen years of age. Williams was now above the middle size, and seemed to have done growing; while Reynolds, on the contrary, seemed as if he had only just begun to grow, and was, as his Aunt Joanna said, "coming on famously." She began to think, after all, that her nephew would, in his way, be every bit as good-looking as Williams. He was stouter built, to be sure, and would never be so tall, but there was such a firm, manly air about him, something so honest and good in his countenance—it was quite a pleasure to look at him!

It was now the middle of winter—a cold, sleety day, when no customers, saving such as wanted physic, turned out of doors. The shop-door was shut, the stove was burning cheerily, and the two apprentices were standing together, looking over a play-bill, which had just been thrown in.

Players were come to the town; a theatre was opened, and that night the performances began. "The Beaux' Stratagem:" it was a charming play, said Williams; and read over the list of characters and performers like a school-boy running over a well-practised lesson. There was nothing in this world that he enjoyed like the theatre; to see a play well acted was the finest thing in the world— the next best thing was to see one badly acted. Oh, a tragedy acted by strolling players, there was something quite racy about it! He declared that he should be a great patron of the theatre. He would take care, he said, and get Mr. Osborne's con-sent to their going.

There was no difficulty about that. Mr. Osborne was the most indulgent of masters; and the two young men set off arm-in-arm, in the highest spirits, intending to be very critical, and yet very much amused.

A great club-room at one of the inns had been converted into a very pretty little theatre, which was well lighted, and tolerably decorated. Neither boxes, pit, nor gallery had one seat to spare; the players evidently had taken the little town at the right moment. Williams, however, was at first amazingly critical; found unmeasured fault, and ridiculed everything. He had seen, he said, in his time, the finest theatres in London, and he knew what good acting was, too. The acting, however, pleased him; above all things, the acting of Miss Jessie Banner-man, who performed the character of Dorinda. He declared that she was a goddess, an angel; so young, not above sixteen; so divinely beautiful! she was equal to any actress in genteel comedy that he had ever seen. He must know something about her! He was very fond of players, he said; loved, of all things, to have the *entrée* of the green-room; had a vast fancy for acting himself; and ended by pro-testing that he was deeply in love with that girl, and would make her acquaintance, or know the reason why.

CHAPTER IV.

JESSIE'S ACQUAINTANCE MADE.

WE must now pay a visit to the house of a clog and patten-maker, and, without using any ceremony, enter the little parlour, which is but very humbly furnished, with its home-made listing carpet hardly covering its brick floor, and its furniture of blue and white check. In the middle of the room stands a round table, covered with a coarse huckaback table-cloth, on which plates, knives and forks, and an earthenware salt-cellar, with bread and cheese, give intimation that supper is at hand. The homely furniture, however, did not cause a moment's uneasiness to the persons who were there, and whom we may as well introduce to the reader. First of all, a little old woman, in a night-cap not remarkably clean, and a pink bed-gown, who sat bending over the little fire-place set in Dutch tile, cooking on the fire a quantity of tripe, in a sauce-pan rather too small for the purpose, while within the fender stood dishes and plates to warm. This old woman, known in the theatrical corps as Mrs. Bellamy, though she never acted, seemed so absorbed by her occupation as to take no notice whatever of a young couple who sat together, in very amicable proximity, on the sofa. These were Jessie Bannerman, the fair *prima donna* of the company, and our acquaintance, Williams, who was now paying by no means his first visit to the inmates of the patten-maker's parlour. Williams was very handsomely dressed in his Sunday clothes, for it was Sunday evening; whilst the young lady, a

slight, delicate young creature, was decidedly *en
déshabillé*, a costume which, although it bore unequi-
vocal marks of having been supplied by a scanty
purse, was not unbecoming to her remarkably interesting appearance.

The youth held both her hands in his, and gazed
with almost devotion into her face. She seemed to
have been weeping, but a faint smile, like April
sunshine, passed at that moment over her face, and
she replied, in answer to some remark of his, "Oh,
no, the dear old creature, she is very deaf; she
hears nothing we say, and if she did, she would not
interrupt us. Ah, she is a good creature!" exclaimed she, snatching away her hands from their
confinement; and starting up to the old woman's
side, she put them on her shoulder, and spoke in
her ear, but not loudly, "I have been telling him
how good you are to me, and how much I love
you," added she, and kissed the old woman's
wrinkled cheek. The old woman understood the
action, if not the words, and gave several little,
short nods, without turning her head, or apparently
lifting her eyes from the saucepan.

The young girl sat down again, and continued,
"If it were not for her, my life would be worse
than that of a galley-slave. She is not as poor as
she seems, and has managed to make herself of
consequence to the company; and Mr. Maxwell,
the manager, consults her in everything. He hates
her, however, for all that, and they quarrel dread-
fully."

Whilst these few words passed, the old woman
had dished her tripe, which she covered up with a
basin, and set within the fender, while she went out

for ale in a small jug. When she returned, and showed what her errand had been, the youth started up, exclaiming against his own forgetfulness, and took from the pocket of his great-coat, which he had laid upon the floor, two bottles of wine, which he said he had brought for them, and which he believed would prove good. The old and the young lady both expressed surprise, and then they all three sat down to supper with the most apparent cordiality. The old woman's tripe was excellent, and well cooked, and Williams's wine was as good as need be drunk; but here, before it could be drunk, there occurred a little difficulty. The wine-glasses of the patten-maker's wife were locked up in a corner-cupboard of this room; she would not entrust her keys to her lodgers, nor would they admit her into the room, lest she should recognise Mr. Osborne's apprentice, whom she well knew, in the young visitor who usually came in so muffled up and disguised that he passed for one of. the players themselves. Two little china cups, therefore, that stood on the mantel-piece. as ornaments, were substituted instead; the old woman having one to herself, and Jessie and her lover—for lover he was —the other between them. After supper, which all three had seemed greatly to enjoy, the old woman swept up the hearth, cleared away the supper-things, and sticking the corks into the bottles, lest, as she said, such good wine should spoil, seated herself in a low-armed chair, and, throwing her apron over her face, lay back as if to sleep; whilst Jessie and the young man resumed their seats on the sofa, and shortly afterwards fell into deep conversation.

"And must I tell you all?" asked she.

"All, every incident from your earliest memory," returned he, passionately. "Whatever concerns you, interests me."

Jessie heaved a deep sigh, and was silent for a few moments.

"I have heard *her* say," at length she began, looking towards the old woman in the chair opposite, "that my mother was the most beautiful of women, and perhaps, also, the most unfortunate. She was the daughter of a village schoolmaster, a man possessed of some little property; and *she*," said she, again indicating the old woman opposite, "was, I fancy, his wife, and consequently is my grandmother; but that she never will confess, although I have besought her on my knees. My mother was loved, or rather courted, by a rich gentleman. She loved him—oh, too well: he deserted her, and her father, who was a very severe, although in his way a very religious man, never would forgive her error. He turned her, one wild autumn night, out of doors. It thundered and lightened, and was a night on which to lose one's senses, or else to do some horrid deed. Her mother prayed the father to relent, and to open the door; for she stayed wandering about the house till long after midnight, begging and praying that he would not be so hard-hearted and so cruel—but it was all in vain! He was one of those men who think that it was the woman only who fell; he thought that the man was a superior being, whose place in creation was to domineer over woman, and punish her, and subject her as much as he could. It was a sort of virtue in his eyes, and so he neither would listen to the prayers of his wife nor daughter."

"What a monster he was!" exclaimed Williams, in a very audible voice.

The old woman put her apron from her head, and said sharply to him, "It is fine talking, young man! but you are all tyrants by nature—every one of you —for all you look so mild and gentle! Every one of you!" added she, again throwing her apron over her head.

"I thought that she was deaf!" exclaimed Williams, amazed, and almost terrified.

"And so she is," returned Jessie, "but you are so violent."

"Well, go on," said he; "your story affects me."

"My grandfather," continued she, "would not go to bed till long after my mother's voice had ceased outside, and then he took the key of the house-door and put it under his pillow, to prevent his wife going out. She was very much afraid of her husband, so she waited till she heard him snoring in bed, and then she got out at the kitchen-window; but nowhere could she find her daughter. She wandered about all day, and went into the neighbours' barns, and up and down the river-side; but she found no traces, nor had anybody in the village seen her. Towards evening, however, she met a wagoner coming with his team towards the village, who had been out with barley to a neighbouring town; and from him she learnt that, about three o'clock in the morning, he had overtaken a young woman, who was walking alone on the road, and who seemed very much distressed. She begged him, he said, to give her a lift in his wagon, which he did; he had also

4

given her part of the refreshment which he had
with him for himself, and had spoken a good word
for her to the woman of the house where he put
up; but that, after she left his wagon, which was
at the town's end, he had seen no more of her, nor
could he tell what it was her intention to do, or
where to go.   My grandmother was so affected by
this mark of kindness, especially, as she said, in a
man, that she thought within herself, what could
she give him in return.   She felt in her pocket, but
money she had none, excepting a crooked Queen
Anne's sixpence with a hole through it, which she
had kept many years.   This she gave to him, and
begged of him to keep for her sake; and for her
sake, also, to be kind to poor women whenever he
met with them, and to take her blessing for the
kindness he had shown her daughter.   Instead of
going home, she at once turned herself round, and
walked through the night back to the town, where
she arrived at daybreak.   The woman of the
public-house could give no information respecting
her daughter, so at night she set off home again."

"She spent that day, and the next, and the next
after that," said the old woman rapidly, interrupting
her, and throwing the apron from her face, and
sitting up in the chair; "three whole days she
spent in searching for her daughter!   It was a
large town, and a wicked town, and nothing but sin,
and misery, and sorrow, did she meet with everywhere, wherever she sought for her poor outcast!
But she did not find her!   Many a fair young
creature she saw, as desolate as her own child; but
her own child she found not, and, with a bleeding,
downcast heart, and a weary body, she retraced her

steps homeward. Her husband, as she came back, sat among the little boys in the school just as if nothing had happened, and heard them read about Mary Magdalene, in the Bible, that our Lord and Saviour Jesus Christ himself had mercy on, yet he never had pity on his own flesh and blood! If I were to tell you," continued she, " of the tears, and the heart-aches, and the prayers of that mother, all in secret between her Maker and herself, you, that are young, would maybe not believe me, so I pass them all over. In a winter or two afterwards, her husband got a rheumatic fever, and she then had to wait on him night and day : he was as helpless as a child, and was cross, and out of humour with her, and with himself, too. She had a weary life of it. The parson came to see him, and preachers of all sorts, from far and near; for he was reckoned a religious man; and being parish schoolmaster, and a man of property besides, folks thought much of him, and his wife got them to talk to him of his daughter, now that he was sick and helpless, and turn his heart towards her, if they could. But he was as hard as iron, and he would not even have her mentioned in his prayers. Well, it pleased God to afflict him in many ways, and he had fits and spasms, and was speechless for months.

" 'Stephen,' said his wife to him, one night, 'God is punishing you for your hardness to poor Mary. You deserve it ! and I hope he will never take his hand off you till you've forgiven her, and acted as a Christian should do !'

" He had not spoken for months and months, and you may think what was her surprise when he lifts himself slowly up in bed, and fixing his hollow eyes on her, says, ' He *has* punished me—punished me severely. I forgive her, and may God Almighty forgive us both!' With these words he dropped back on the pillow, and his poor wife was so over-come by what she heard, all so unexpectedly, that she sank down as if she had been smitten, and when she had strength to rise again—he was a corpse! A bitter feeling now came over her towards herself: she had been angry with him—she had done her duty to him only as duty, not as love. What would she not have given then for one week, one hour, of his past life! Ah, children, children!" said she, addressing the two before her, "never grieve those you love; never lose an opportunity of doing a kindness to those you love; never give way to bitterness and hardness, else you will lay up a punishment for yourselves which will pursue you as with a whip of scorpions!".

A silence of a few minutes ensued. Jessie had thrown herself back in a corner of the sofa, and Williams sat staring at the old woman, who now, as if with all her faculties awake, continued :—

"Some indistinct rumour reached the mother, some time after her husband's death, that her daughter was in London; so she turned all the little property that was left into money, and to London she went. She went to London to find her daughter. And how was her daughter to be found among the thousands of other women's daughters, that were outcasts in society—women with beauty, talents, affections, all trampled under foot, viler than the very mud of the streets! She went out on the evenings of summer days, when the birds of heaven were singing, and the dew lay as pure as angels' thoughts on the grassy fields; and what did she meet? Women that the rich and pampered daughters of untempted virtue loathed; but she met not with her daughter. She went out on cold, desolate, pinching nights of winter, when happy families sat round happy hearths—fathers, and mothers, and little children, and blessed God that they lived in a Christian land, where all misery was cared for; and what did she still meet? Poor, unfortunate women again—creatures that God had made a little lower than the angels; for what? To be the prey of the vilest passions of man; to be despised, scorned, pointed at, trampled on; to be miserable and outcast! These she saw, winter and summer, alike; these, beauty and misery, going hand-in-hand down to the pit! Yes, young man," said she, lifting up an admonitory finger, "such as you it is that do this work of death and the devil! and think not that you shall come here, paying your flattering, false attentions to that old woman's grand-daughter unwatched and unprevented!"

"Upon my soul," said the young man, quite taken by surprise, "I am sincere as the very sun in heaven! Only, you see, as yet, I am in trammels; I am not my own master."

"Enough! enough!" said the old woman. "But I have not yet done. You asked for Jessie's history, and we are not yet come to it. I had been out one night to get a bit of butcher's-meat; I had not had a bit for months, and somehow or other the fancy took me to have a bit; so I went out that Saturday night, and had not gone far, before I was stopped by a crowd at the door of a house, where they said that a man was ill-using a woman. 'It's *only* his wife!' said somebody near me; just as if he had said, it's only his dog. These were things that I felt in my very soul; so I rushed into the house, just as the brutal husband, mad with liquor and cruelty, and with blood upon his clothes, threw himself out of the door into the middle of the crowd, which, 'spite of the attempts to seize upon him, he struck off right and left, and made his escape. A crowd of people beside me had rushed into the house, and up-stairs where the woman was, whose blood we met, trickling down-stairs, before we reached the top. She was bleeding from face, and neck, and arms, where she had many great gashes. She looked as if she were already dead, and a little child, not six months old, lay crying on the miserable bed beside her. The sight of the woman caused a cry of indignation and horror in the people, and half of them turned back to overtake and secure the man whom they now regarded as a murderer. From a feeling of pity which wrung my very heart, I took up the child in my arms; it looked into my face, and smiled! It was *she!*" said the old woman, pointing to Jessie, who now, pale and excited, was weeping again.

"They took the woman to the hospital," continued she. "She was one of a travelling company of comedians and horse-riders; her husband and she acted the principal parts: she had been, and still was, very beautiful. She was the schoolmaster's daughter — the daughter of that mother who had sought her so long and so wearily! She did not die. There were two children: the infant, and a girl of seven years old, a young creature that played night after night, and was the great attraction of the company. She was ill, and it had been about her acting that the parents had quarrelled that night. She was a wonderful child. Oh, why are such gifts as hers given, when they can lead but to misery and ruin! The little Fanny danced on the tight-rope night after night, and performed the most wonderful feats of horsemanship as the Flying Circassian; and acted and sung to the delight of crowds of thoughtless, admiring people. She played, and danced, and rode, and grew weaker and weaker day by day; but there was no pity either for her or the infant, which, as soon as it could walk, was made to ride and dance, and which promised to be as great a prodigy as her sister. When the mother was dead, I joined myself to the company. The father hated me, but he could not get rid of me. I stayed, because there was no law to take them forcibly from the father. After I had been with the company some years, things mended. All were not as bad as he; poor they all were, but many of them had kind hearts, and there were those with us who would take our parts; and besides, as Fanny's health mended under my care, the father no longer tried to make my life intolerable; besides which, a cold which I took made me deaf, so that I could not hear him. He married again, and then I took the children to myself; the travelling life was not unpleasant to me, and Fanny was a very angel."

"And where is Fanny?" asked Williams. The old woman made no reply.

Jessie took the handkerchief from her face, and laying her hand on his arm, said solemnly, "Fanny is dead!"

He looked shocked, and she continued, "Had

you known Fanny, you would never have loved me. I am no more to be compared to her, than the moon to the sun. She was nineteen when she died; I was then twelve. *She,*" said she, pointing to the old woman, "had much more reason to love Fanny than me. She was much handsomer than me, and was so witty and merry! Ill as she was, it never cast her down; and her laugh! Oh, I remember it now! I never heard a laugh like it— so sweet, so joyous, so musical! My father used to say that her laugh would make her fortune; but she took cold one night at the theatre, and in three days she died! They think of making another Fanny of me," said she; " but it will not do. My father is disappointed in me. I am not as brilliant as my sister. My life is not happy—not at all happy," said she, clasping her hands, and bursting into a passion of tears.

"Adorable girl!" said Williams, quite beside himself with love and pity, and throwing himself on one knee before her. "My whole life shall be devoted to making your life happy!"

The fair Jessie bowed her face, and wept upon his shoulder.

"Hey-day!" said the old woman, starting up from her chair, " what nonsense is all this! I know what it means when men talk of life-long devotion. And what are *you*, young man? Can *you* rescue her from the life of misery that lies before her?"

"I am one who love her better than life," said Williams, starting to his feet, and facing the old woman with quite a theatrical air. "I love her, and, were I but free, I would marry her to-morrow."

"Fine talking!" said the old woman, with a

sneer; "*if I were but free!* that is always the way! *If I were but free, indeed!* Why, when you are free, your mind will have changed. Then, then! ah, I know you men! You are a pack of designing, selfish knaves, and I'll have none of you! I'll take care of Jessie Bannerman, if she cannot take care of herself; and so you had better take your leave, for the decent people at your house must have been in bed these two or three hours."

"By Jove, and so they will!" exclaimed Williams, looking at his watch, and horrified to see that it was past two o'clock.

"I shall never get in to-night," said he, almost dolefully. "For Heaven's sake let me sleep where I am. I will lie on the sofa, or anywhere, and early in the morning I will be gone."

The old woman was again deaf; and it was only by his forcibly taking possession of the sofa, that she seemed to understand him. Jessie laughed as merrily and as musically, Williams thought, as Fanny could have done, and applauded the idea. But the old woman was inexorable, and turned him literally out of doors.

Well was it for him that, in that quiet town, every soul, excepting the watchman, was in bed. The night was fine and starlight, and avoiding the watchman, who made himself perceptible by his cry, he walked through the town right into the country, which was not inconvenient to him, as he had excused his yesterday's absence on the plea of spending the afternoon with some friends in the country; and the next morning he entered Mr. Osborne's parlour just as they were about to sit down to breakfast, nobody suspecting one word of the real truth.

CHAPTER V.

A SPOKE IN THE WHEEL.

My readers may imagine how confusing must have been all the inquiries which assailed the young man from Mrs. Osborne during breakfast. "Well, and how were the Yates's? Is he better? and is John come from Birmingham? And what news have they from Mrs. Benjamin? Are the children better? And has Jenny had the measles?"

Williams was not a young man to be easily dumb-foundered; his replies really were all so straight-forward, that nobody could have had the slightest suspicion of all not being quite straightforward regarding them. All this, however, was nothing to the difficulty he found after breakfast, when he was told to assist in the putting up of a large order for a country-shop. What room had he in his mind for 6 lbs. of yellow ochre, and 2 lbs. of camomile flowers, and glue, and lamp-black, and syrup of squills, and opium?

"What, are not those things put up yet?" asked Mr. Osborne, looking down into the lower ware-house, as he saw Williams by lamplight, towards dinner-time, weighing out whitening, which he knew came fourth in a list of seven-and-twenty articles. No, indeed! they were not put up. Williams had thought of nothing all the morning but the fair Jessie, and her sad family history, and her deaf old grand-mother, who, after all, was not deaf. He went over the history, incident by incident, and asked himself many questions. Who, then, was Jessie's father? Was it that Mr. Maxwell, the manager, with whom she had said that the old woman often quarrelled? and if so, why was she called Bannerman? Was that her mother's name? and if so, why, then, was the old woman called Bellamy? He could not understand these things. One thing, however, he could very well understand, and that was, that he was desperately in love; should never love anybody else as long as he lived; and if he were but out of his time would marry her instantly, even if he had to starve all the rest of his life for it.

What an awkward thing it is for a young man violently in love, and a little headstrong into the bargain, not to be out of his time—not to be at liberty to do just as he likes! He grew quite desperate there, down among the whitening casks and the hogsheads of oil and vinegar. He remembered her tears, and that she had declared herself to be unhappy; and that she had to display all her charms and her powers of pleasing every night to worthless crowds, whilst he was dying but for one glance of hers. And then, how did he know but that some young fellow who was "out of his time," and his own master, might not fall in love with her, and carry her off at once! What so likely? He then laid a thousand impossible plans, which at the moment he vowed to execute. He would join the company, and travel with her. He would run off with her, and get married; his uncle and aunt would be angry, he knew, but in the end they would forgive him. Jessie should throw herself at their feet; they could never withstand her beauty and her tears. In 'the midst of this scene he was woke to reality and a dinner of boiled beef and turnips. Poor Williams! he had no appetite, and he looked as woe-begone as it was possible for any young apprentice to look who was over head and ears in love. He was not well, he said; he was, to use the words of a country swain in love, "hot and dry, like, with a pain in his side, like;" and he prescribed for himself a walk in the fresh air, which Mr. Osborne freely permitted to him. deputing Reynolds to finish his work below.

Williams dressed himself with great care, and putting on his great-coat, made the best of his way to the clog and patten-maker's, not failing to see, as he passed along the streets, on every blank wall and every projecting house-corner, the name of his fair one in the play-bills for the night, " To be performed this evening, the Fair Quaker of Deal, the part of the Fair Quaker, by Miss Jessie Bannerman." Jessie was the attraction of the company—the whole town acknowledged it. The sight of her name added to his impatience; he reached the house, and thinking neither of the patten-maker nor his wife, rushed through the kitchen, where they sat at tea, without any precaution of concealment, and knocking hurriedly at the parlour-door, entered without waiting for permission from within.

" Why, that's Osborne's smart apprentice, for sure," exclaimed the patten-maker's wife; " so, he's smitten, is he, with that young player-wench ? "

" Why, how many young chaps are there after her ? " asked her husband.

" Half-a-score," said the wife, "at least;" and began counting them on her fingers.

Williams's entrance produced quite a sensation among the three persons in the room. The old woman, who sat with her spectacles on, sewing

white muslin cuffs into the slate-coloured stuff gown
which was evidently to be the dress of the Fair
Quaker of Deal, knocked down an old pasteboard
box which held her store of sewing materials. Jessie,
who stood *en déshabillé*, as yesterday, with her little
Quaker's cap in her hand, turned first red and then
pale at the sight of him; and a tall young man, of
perhaps two-and-twenty, who was at that moment
presenting her with a bouquet of splendid greenhouse flowers, started back a step or two, as if a
snake had stung him, and then stood, with the flowers
in his hand, and a look of defiance in his eye, at the
unexpected rival, whom the lady might be supposed
to favour from her changing colour. A glance told
all this; and Williams, on his part, looked as much
taken by surprise as any of them. Here had he
flown on the wings of love and impatience only to
find a rival—a favoured rival his jealousy whispered,
and that in the handsome person of Tom Bassett, a
young man of family—an articled clerk of the first
lawyer in the place;—he was in love with her too—
it was death and destruction!

"Shall you see me to-night as the Fair Quaker?"
asked Jessie, with one of her sweetest smiles.

"Most certainly I shall," said Williams, who, in
the face of his rival, felt that it must be so.

She showed him the cap, and pointed to the dress
which the old woman was engaged upon for the
character; and while he turned to speak to the old
woman, who seemed now deafer than ever, Tom
Bassett again presented his flowers, which were
graciously accepted. Williams did not wait for the
old woman's answer, but was, the same moment.
at Jessie's side again, looking daggers at the free-and-

5

easy young lawyer. With the air of a queen, Jessie motioned the two to be seated. Bassett laughed and talked with the most provoking ease and confidence. In his eyes, evidently, Williams was a rival not worth noticing. Jessie laughed at his jokes, and seemed not to trouble herself about the other. It was mortifying, it was provoking, it was enough to make a saint swear, thought Williams. "Here I sit," thought he to himself, "like a fool, without a word to say for myself!" If he *were* to speak, he knew that his voice would betray his feelings—he wished his rival at the devil. We beg our readers' pardon, but it is truth; he did so, and he wished more than that—that he could challenge him, and put a bullet through his body. It was a most uncomfortable time to him. He called Bassett an ass—a stupid, conceited ass—in his own mind; and perhaps he might have been excited to call him so to his face, if the old woman, who had finished her work, had not got up, and shaking out the gown, said it was now ready, and as it was five o'clock, the gentlemen had better both take their departure. "Did they hear?" she repeated, as if she thought them as deaf as herself.

They both rose, and Jessie offering a hand to each at the same moment, curtseyed them a graceful adieu.

"I *must* say a word to you," whispered Williams, as Bassett left the room.

"To-night, after the play. I do not act in the after-piece," said she, hurriedly, and closed the door upon him. But that was enough; he wanted no more; he felt as if wings had at once sprung from his shoulders.

The patten-maker sold tickets for the play, and the words that he heard after the parlour-door had shut were, " ten box-tickets for to-night."

The patten-maker counted out the tickets, and Bassett, who had drawn forth a handsome scarlet purse with gold rings from his pocket, laid down a guinea, and without waiting for the change, drew on his gloves, and pocketed his purse and the tickets.

" Ten box-tickets," said Williams to the patten-maker, who looked as if he had expected it ; and thinking of a bootmaker's bill, for the payment of which he had received money from his aunt, drew forth a very modest little brown purse, which Miss Dorothy Kendrick had netted for him, and paid for his tickets with a half-guinea, a half-crown, five shillings, and four sixpences ; the coin looked quite beggarly, and the purse was left so empty that the rings slid off as he put it again into his pocket. But he was not going to trouble himself just then on that subject. Tom Bassett also stood on the door-step as he went out, and drawing forth an eye-glass, contemptuously surveyed him from head to foot. Eye-glasses, in those days, were not as common as now ; and Williams, though he felt stung, as it were, from head to heel, hummed, with a gallant, careless toss of the head, one of Jessie's favourite airs ; and recollecting how inconvenient any public quarrel would be, or, in fact, any quarrel at all, as it would bring more than he liked to the knowledge of his uncle, turned upon his heel and walked down the street.

Now came the consideration respecting the ten tickets, and he almost thought himself a fool for having bought more than one for himself. What

was he now to do with them ? He walked across
the fields towards the Dove-Bridge, and came to the
very wise conclusion, that two of them he would
keep, and the other eight, wrapping neatly in paper,
he would drop, on his return, in the market-place,
where they would be sure to be found. As to the
two that ne retained, he would boldly confess the
having purchased them, and ask permission for
Reynolds and himself to go to the theatre that night.
He did as he had resolved ; and, after just abouι
as much reproof as he expected from Mr. and Mrs.
Osborne, tea was hastened, and, grateful to his companion for having obtained for him this unexpected
pleasure, Reynolds ran up-stairs to prepare his
toilet.

The little theatre was crowded, and the fair Jessie
was received most enthusiastically. Williams thought
her lovelier than ever in her quiet Quaker costume.
"All the town is in love with her," said he to his
companion; "and is she not an angel ?"

It was quite a brilliant night. The very gentry of
the town were there ; and there, seated between the
two daughters of the lawyer, sat Tom Bassett.
Williams was delighted, for with these two young
ladies he was quite secure for the night.

"And now, my dear, good fellow," whispered
Williams to his companion, just before the curtain
fell, " you must stand my friend. You will; promise
me you will !" said he, laying his hand on his arm,
and looking quite agitated. " I am in love with
Miss Bannerman ; she knows it ; she loves me, too,
and has promised me a little interview this evening.
She is a very angel : she is a good girl, I assure you !
I love her as my life, and I am sure you will be my

friend. She does not act again to-night," continued he, rapidly, and not allowing Reynolds time to speak, "but you will stay the after-piece—it is the most amusing thing in the world; and if I am not at home by the time you are, don't let anybody miss me— and I'll do as much for you any time!"

"But, Williams," began he. Williams, however, did not wait to hear. The curtain fell, and he was gone.

He knew perfectly the back-entrance by which Jessie would leave the theatre; and there, at the very moment of time, stood she, wrapped in a cloak, and attended by the old woman with a lighted lantern. 'Spite of the lawyer's daughters, there also was Bassett, making a thousand protestations of regret and chagrin at not being able to accompany her.

"She wants no escort," said Williams, rendered bold by his good fortune; "I shall have that happiness," and taking Jessie's little hand, which he drew within his arm, he walked off triumphantly.

"The jackanapes! the conceited jackanapes!" exclaimed Bassett; but not imagining for a moment that Jessie would give a druggist's apprentice the preference over him, he went back to the theatre laughing to himself at the youth's "ignorant conceit."

Williams walked off triumphantly with Jessie on his arm, and the little old woman trudged beside them with her lantern; but scarcely had they gone ten yards when they were stopped by a man who put a small paper into their hands.

What had they here? They stopped; and, by the light of the lantern, read the words. printed in great, black, awful-looking letters, "The Doors of the Play-house lead to Hell!"

" It 's the parson's doing!" said Williams, shocked
at what he had read aloud, and crumpling it in his
hand, threw it from him.   " He is a narrow-souled,
bigoted, methodistical fellow, who sets his face
against every kind of pleasure!   It is just like him!"

This little incident, however, seemed to throw no
gloom on him, after the first moment; so, leaving
them to their full enjoyment, we will return to Reynolds, who was thrown, by his companion's sudden
desertion, into a state of the most complete perplexity.
Reynolds was a good-hearted fellow; he always
looked upon Williams as much older in worldly
experience than he was; he, himself, was a child in
comparison of him, a mere apprentice; whilst the
other had been, as it were, " out of his time" this many
and many a day.   He had long known that Williams
would never excel in his business; he had neglected
the study of every branch of it ever since the first
glow of novelty was worn off.   He was frank in his
confession about it; he hated business, and would
never do any more than he was obliged; yet the
impulses of his nature were often good and kind; he
knew his own weaknesses and acknowledged them,
and was quite willing that Reynolds should stand
a long way before him in the good opinion of Mr.
Isaacs.   Reynolds really liked him, and had so con-
stantly and for so long done his work, and hidden
all his misdemeanors, and made up for his shortcomings, that Williams had the fullest confidence
that he would befriend him also in this instance.
Betray him he never would; and he'would smuggle
him, safely and unseen, into the house, if he sate up
the whole night for it.   Yes; that was all true.   But
for all that, Reynolds was not at all pleased with the

position he was now placed in. This, then, was
what he had been brought for; he had been made
a cat's-paw of, and he felt vexed; besides this, he
was very honourable and religious in his principles
and notions; and the hurried and candid confession
of his companion had utterly shocked and confounded
him. For his part, he would as soon have thought
of falling in love with his grandmother as with a
player—for so he called her, not "actress," as
Williams did, let her be as beautiful as she might:
and then to make appointments with her at night;—
there was something quite frightful to him in it.
And all at once the whole scene before him lost its
attraction. It was a wicked place! that which they
had just seen performed was low and disgusting—a
burlesque, a coarse caricature! He was offended
—ashamed—angry with himself for having been
amused;—and now this "after-piece" was worse
and worse—there was not even the beauty of Jessie
Bannerman to set it off; the women were painted,
gaudy creatures; the men fit associates for them.

It was in this spirit that Reynolds sat out the
"after-piece."

When the company dispersed from the theatre,
there was not *one* man but *three* who distributed their
little printed papers. Everybody had one, some two
or three; and everybody, on reading them, exclaimed
—"This is Mr. Goodman's doing;" or "This is the
parson's doing;" or "We shall have a sermon against
the players on Sunday."

And all these exclamations were right. There
was a sermon against them on Sunday, and a severe
one, too; and not alone against players and play-
houses, but against all playgoers, also. But before

Sunday, the clergyman, who was one of the best of men, although one of the most rigid, called on the Osbornes, as he had been doing for some days on his delinquent flock, to remonstrate with so respectable a man, and so good a church-goer as Mr. Osborne, on allowing his apprentices to frequent places of such awful wickedness as theatres!

Williams was faint with apprehension lest the clergyman knew also of his passion and his acquaintance with the fair Jessie; the patten-maker and his wife knew of it; Tom Bassett knew of it; oh, it must come out! He felt quite ill, and went into the upper warehouse, looking like anything but a bold lover, where he sat down on a resin-tub, waiting for the judgment which he feared might be at hand.

Mr. Osborne was a very good, kind-hearted man, good to the poor, and charitable in the gospel-sense of the word to all mankind. He thought players bad, low people; but, for his part, he saw no use in commencing a crusade against them. We should never exterminate them, they would exist 'spite of us; and people, he said, would go to theatres to be amused. People must be amused; he saw no harm in it at all. He had had some thoughts, he said, of going himself; and as to his apprentices—why, if his young men were good and steady, and attended to their business, he thought it only right now and then to give them a bit of pleasure. He had always done so; he had been forty years in business; had had about seven-and-twenty apprentices, all of whom, for what he knew, had turned out well. He thought that was a proof that his system was not a very bad one; and with all respect for the clergyman, whom nobody respected more than he did, he must still be allowed to pursue his own course.

The clergyman used his strongest arguments; he knew nothing as yet of Williams's affairs, or he would have had a famous argument in his hand; but still Mr. Osborne adhered to the very last to his own opinions—perhaps even went a little beyond them in opposition to what seemed the ultra opinions of the other.

All this went on in the parlour, and Mr. Isaacs and a customer, who was of the clergyman's way of thinking, discussed the subject in the shop, whilst Reynolds went on with his weighing and labelling and pill-making, and thinking that they were right, every word they said. He did believe all players, men, women, and children, to be a wicked, low, dissolute, unprincipled set of people, and it was not his intention ever to go near them again.

Next morning, before church, came Miss Joanna Kendrick to beg that her nephew might go to church. She was warmer even than the clergyman had been, and really censured Mr. Osborne for letting his young men go to the play-house. If *she* had been asked, she said, she should have prevented it, at least as far as her nephew was concerned. Mr. Osborne could do just as he liked with regard to the other.

Mr. Osborne felt quite vexed—for the first time in his life vexed with Miss Kendrick. He repeated to her what he had said to the clergyman about his forty years' experience in business and the management of apprentices; but it was quite in another tone of voice, and Miss Kendrick was hurt. She replied warmly, and so did he; and really these two excellent people might have quite come to a quarrel had not a note at that moment, from a physician, required Mr. Osborne's particular attention.

This note was an awkward affair, indeed; such a thing as this had never occurred before in the whole forty years of Mr. Osborne's practice. He started up, and, with the note in his hand, went into the back-room, which was appropriated to Mr. Isaacs and the young men.

" Who made up that prescription of Dr. Chawner's, yesterday?" asked he.

Mr. Isaacs considered for a moment, and then replied that Williams had done it.

Williams was sitting there reading a volume of Massinger's plays, which he had borrowed from Anderson, one of the actors; he started, and looked frightened. " Why, what of the prescription?" he asked.

" Did you make that up yesterday?" asked Mr. Osborne, in an angry tone.

" I did, sir," he returned, submissively.

" And how came you, then, to put in 40 drops tinctura opii and 6 tinctura scillæ, instead of 6 drops tinctura opii and 40 tinctura scillæ?"

Williams could not tell, unless he had mistaken it.

Mr. Osborne swore—yes, actually on a Sunday morning. Williams's answer had provoked him to it. " Mistaken a physician's prescription! What the deuce did he mean by mistaking a physician's prescription, or anything else! He would be poisoning people some of these days; what had he learnt his business for," &c., &c.

Never had Mr. Osborne, in all his forty years' practice, been so angry as then. It was the first

time in his life that ever a mistake had been made at
his counter in a physician's prescription.

Williams knew well enough the cause of his
blunder—he knew where his thoughts had been
when he made up the prescription.   He had not a
word to say for himself.

Mr. Isaacs, almost as vexed as Mr. Osborne, made
up the prescription, vowing with himself that he
never would put another into Williams's hands.
Mr. Osborne wrote the best apology he could to the
physician, and Williams sat all the morning reading
Massinger's plays.

CHAPTER VI.

DEEPER AND DEEPER.

THE whole town talked of nothing but the players.
One half the inhabitants sided with the clergyman,
the other half with Mr. Maxwell's company.   The
theatrical party was headed by the family of the
lawyer with whom was Tom Bassett; and this same
lawyer not only bespoke a play, but talked of giving
a supper to the principal performers.

The lawyer's daughters thought of nothing but
private theatricals; and Tom Bassett, who was hand
and glove with half the theatrical staff, as well as
desperately in love with the prima donna, borrowed
the actors' own copies of plays, and was *au fait* in
all that appertained to theatrical life.

On the other hand, among the persons most active
on the side of the clergyman, were the good Miss
Kendricks.   It was as good as a sermon to hear
Miss Joanna talk; she really was more effective than

the clergyman, because she was less violent. He talked of the theatre as the "devil's house," called theatricals the "work of hell," and denounced all such as, after thus being warned, wilfully aided and abetted them, "as heirs of damnation." It was quite awful to hear him talk. Miss Joanna, on the contrary, spoke in love and tenderness, pitied the "poor, benighted creatures," the players; who, she said, were more to be lamented over than pagan Hottentots, and she besought people, for the love of their own souls, not to give them encouragement; nor would she at all go the length that the clergyman did, in saying that it would be a good thing if every copy of Shakspeare had been burned publicly by the hand of the hangman. No, Miss Joanna, in all her zeal, talked like a tender-hearted Christian, and people listened to her. But, spite of all that she said, and spite of all the clergyman thundered forth, the little theatre was crowded night after night.

Mr. Maxwell, the red-faced manager, said that he liked nothing so well as the opposition of a parson; it always did the house good, and he did not know whether he should not introduce Mr. Goodman some night on the stage.

All this time the rivalry between Tom Bassett and our apprentice went on as hotly as ever. Each thought himself the favoured lover, yet still each hated and feared the other. Between these two young men, however, there was one great difference. Bassett had plenty of money, Williams had none. All that he had of his own had long been gone; the pound that had been given to him by his aunt to pay the poor bootmaker had been spent in tickets, as we know. He had borrowed since then every farthing of money from Reynolds, and which, being but a scanty allowance, was always hoarded and husbanded with the greatest economy. From Mr. Isaacs he dared not borrow; nor, just then, when the memory of his blunder was fresh in his mind, durst he ask money from his uncle. There was, however, the cash in the shop-safe. His uncle placed the greatest confidence in him as regarded money—a great deal more than Mr. Isaacs had done for a long time.

"Shall I or shall I not?" questioned he with himself. Oh, how bad it is when we begin to parley with principle!

"No, I will not!" said he; but he said it feebly, as if he were not at all sure—as if he wanted, if he could, to deceive himself into a notion of his own virtue. "No, I will not!" said he, again and again —"at least, not to-day!" he should have added, to be quite honest to himself.

The next week was Christmas week, and it had been long an understood thing that Williams was to have a holiday on Christmas-day: he ventured to mention it to Mr. Osborne, spite of the unpleasant memory of the prescription. He had heard, he said, how beautiful the gardens at Alton Towers looked in the winter, with snow on the ground and hoar-frost on the trees; he hoped he might be permitted to go there on Christmas-day. "He would be very industrious," he said, "in future;" and being once on the subject, he launched out freely. "He was so sorry, so ashamed," he said, "of the blunder he had made. Mr. Osborne had touched him so by his patience and forbearance." Mr. Osborne, himself, thought that he had not shown much; but so the young man said—"and would he only grant him this

favour now, he would show how grateful he was."
On Mr. Osborne — plain, honest, straight-forward
man as he was, and with every tendency to the indulgence of his nephew,—all this made the very
impression which was desired. "Poor fellow,"
thought he, "he is so cut up about that blunder;
he has never looked like himself since—seems all in
a tremble and a dream; one must not be too severe
with him!"

"Yes, surely, he might go;" but Mr. Osborne
could not imagine how there would be any pleasure
in going alone—could not Reynolds, too, have a holiday? Williams, who did not by any means think
of taking a companion like Reynolds, reminded
Mr. Osborne that Mr. Isaacs went out on Christmas-
day, too, and Reynolds was to have his holiday on
Christmas-eve with his aunts

Miss Kendricks had not been to the Osbornes' since
the little rencontre on Sunday morning; both they
and the Osbornes still let the little affair rankle in
their minds. It was that sort of quarrel which
sometimes the merest trifle occasions between friends,
and whether it shall be healed, or whether it shall
become a wide and lasting breach, depends upon one
or other of them on the first occasion of anxiety or
sorrow. As yet, however, that occasion had not
presented itself, and Reynolds went to spend Christmas-eve with his aunts without being the bearer of
any message from Mrs. Osborne. Such a thing had
never happened before. The Osbornes, also, were
spending Christmas-eve out, and nobody was left at
home but Mr. Isaacs and Williams.

With Williams it seemed as if the crisis of his fate
were come; he had formed his own plans both for

that evening and the morrow; as far as regarded that evening, he had formed them in counsel with himself and in desperation, and to the stifling of the voice of conscience within him. "But what must be, must," said he; "go there with her I must and shall, and to go I must have money."

His plans were, therefore, formed. Reynolds was out of the way; his uncle was so, too; and he made himself sedulously useful in the shop; he made pills, and mixed emulsions for coughs and sold boxes of issue-plaisters, and moved here and there with such alacrity as astonished and delighted poor Mr. Isaacs, who was racked that evening with toothache.

"Go and sit down by the parlour-fire," said Williams, as the time for shutting up the shop approached, "I'll make up the books and see that all is left straight, and you go and make yourself comfortable."

Mr. Isaacs, well pleased to leave his post at the desk, where a draught of cold air came in keenly against his ailing tooth, went into the back-parlour, and Williams had the shop all to himself. The warehouse-boy put up the shutters, raked out the fire, and was dismissed for the night. Williams added up the day-book, counted the money in the till, put three-and-sixpence in his pocket, and entered the amount, minus this, in the day-ledger; and then, unlocking the shop-safe with a trembling hand, looked this way and that, and thought if Isaacs should come in, or if Mr. Osborne should be returning early by some chance, and peep through a crack of the shutters. Oh, that miserable if! But why was he so fearful! Alas, because he intended to take money as he had already done from the till.

Once or twice before, Mr. Isaacs had found some deficiency; Mr. Osborne had never even suspected it; he would as soon have thought of his wife robbing him as Williams.

The money was taken and dropped into the waist-coat pocket; the safe was locked, and double-locked. If he could have seen his own face at that moment he would have started. But he did not; and, rallying himself, he put out the shop-lights, and went into the back-parlour, where the candles were burning dimly with long, unsnuffed wicks, for poor Mr. Isaacs was gone to bed.

There was nobody in the room; it was almost a shock to be thus thrown, as it were, upon himself and his own conscience.

"Suppose," thought he to himself, "that, after all, I have only taken silver, two shillings and sixpence; should I then go back and change them, though I know what a horror this stealing is? I wish one had no need to do it!"

He put his hand into his pocket and drew the money forth to the light. It was gold—two guineas and a half. He felt glad that it was so. The next moment Reynolds returned—the gay, laughing, unanxious Reynolds—Williams envied him his light-ness of heart.

The next morning the church-bells rang; the sun shone bright, and the slight covering of snow and hoar-frost was like the festal garment of nature. The houses were decked with holly and ivy, people were moving briskly about—the whole town was merry; even the paupers in the parish workhouse arose that morning with cheerful expectation, for that day they were to have roast-beef and plum-pudding for dinner.

Many people hired horses and gigs that day and drove out into the country, so that there was nothing at all remarkable in the circumstance of old Evans driving one of his miserable hacks, which, however, was made to wear its best looks that day, in one of his smartest gigs, along the high street and half-a-mile beyond the end of the town. Of this nobody took any notice, and it was so contrived, also, that nobody saw Williams, whose great-coat collar stood up above his ears, whilst his hat was slouched over his eyes, assist into the said gig Miss Bannerman, dressed in a dark blue cloak trimmed with fur, and a black velvet bonnet, and then take nis seat beside her, and drive off briskly. On they drove, and presently overtook two other gigs, in which were seated five members, male and female, of the theatrical corps, who, like them, were going to spend the day in the gardens of Alton Towers. But as with these other five persons we have very little to do, we shall drop them for the present, and confine ourselves to our young couple, just as if they were quite alone.

Williams was enraptured with his fair companion. She looked lovelier than ever in that black velvet bonnet ; the walk in the clear winter air had brought a colour to her cheek like that of the June rose. She was, indeed, very lovely—but not with that vulgar loveliness which alone consists of beauty of complexion, hair as dark and glossy as "the raven's wing," and "dark, blue eyes, as soft as those of the dove." These she had, it is true ; but that which constituted the real charm of her countenance was a sentiment of tenderness, calm decision, and truth and love. It was a face to fill with tears the eyes of any beholder capable of appreciating qualities such as these, in a being exposed to every temptation which can assail beauty and taint the delicacy of woman. Jessie Bannerman, though a "player-wench," as half the town called her, was an extraordinary girl. She knew her own personal worth, and her own dignity as a woman, and she made her lovers feel it, too. It is impossible to say what was the peculiar charm which attracted her towards Williams, but to him she had really given her affections ;—this she had never denied, she was really in earnest in her love ;—and Williams was never with her without feeling, as it were, under the influence of a superior nature. He fancied that he adored her, that he would have laid down his life for her : he bought the pleasure of being in her company at the expense of his own probity ; and yet he felt sure all the time that could she have only known this she would have rejected pleasure at such a cost.

Beautiful as were those magnificent gardens, which are said to be laid out on the traditional plan of the hanging gardens of Babylon, the lovers took but little notice of them ; he was engrossed by her, and she by her own thoughts. At length they reached a pavilion, which, lying in the full sunshine, was warm almost as in summer. Here they seated themselves, and Jessie, turning to the young man, said—

"Now, we have had enough of flattery and nonsense—we must talk seriously. You have talked hitherto ; you must now listen to me. My unhappy family history, which you have heard, can only give you the idea of me as of a creature sprung of wretchedness and crime, to whom God has given, for some mysterious purpose, remarkable gifts—gifts worse than useless if I am to become only the poor degraded being which my present life may seem to foretell. But, Edward," said she, fixing her large, calm eyes upon him, "it must not be so; our destinies, after all, are, in great measure, in our own hands; a spirit within tells me so, and that spirit shall be my guide.

"I have many lovers, but how few there are who would marry such a one as me. I speak plainly, Edward, for one of us must do so; and as I have so much more experience in life than you, and understand you better even than you understand yourself, I speak to you openly. You talk of marriage: what nonsense it is of you, who are as yet a boy, and do not know even your own mind! I believe that you love me; but as yet you do not understand me perfectly, for you have seen only that which is idle and trifling in me; but indeed I am capable of much that is good and ennobling and valuable in life."

"Oh, Jessie," said the young man impatiently, and ready to throw himself at her feet, "let us unite our fates at once. I know what you are — I wish you not other than you are—let me rescue you from a fate which is unworthy of you! My aunt is good. When she knows your excellence she will love you as a daughter: they love me, but how much more will they love you!"

"All nonsense," returned Jessie; "you talk like a child, as you are; you, that dare not even let them know of our acquaintance, to talk thus! No, no; we must have patience, and wait for the true time. You must wait for me for five years."

"I will go with you," interrupted Williams; "what is all the world to me without you! I know that I, too, have talents— I would be prompter

even, or candle-snuffer, or anything to be near
you!"

Jessie laughed and shook her head—"That would
never do," said she; "that would not satisfy me.
My father," she continued, "blames me for want of
ambition; but he mistakes me: I *am* ambitious—
ambitious of the greatest good which life can give,
and that is real love and domestic happiness! Not
such love as we act night after night, poor, unreal
love, all tinsel and glitter;—no, no, the love that I
mean is self-denying, long-suffering, unobtrusive, as
free to the poor as to the rich. Oh, Edward, I was
ill not long ago; the company went on without me,
and I and my good grandmother—for such she is—
remained in the house of a poor tailor. Would you
believe it, but it was truly in that house, and with
those humble people, that I first learned what true
love was, and what was the real meaning and worth
of life. Happiness there was a substantial thing, not
dependent on wealth or the world's favour, for of
these they had nothing; not wavering or uncertain,
according to the whim of the moment, but as real
and steadfast as life itself. Love was never talked of,
but they dwelt in its spirit; it was as if the atmo-
sphere of a better region filled the house; the children
were born in it, and breathed it as their native air,
and they were good and kind like their parents. A
light then broke in upon my mind. My grandmother
saw and felt these things as I did;—she is not,
Edward, the deaf, stupid old woman which it is her
will to appear; but that is her secret—she and I
understand each other. The goal which I have set
before my ambition is a home of love, and my prayers,
Heaven knows, are, that I may be kept pure and

made worthy of it. This is, perhaps, my religion : in the eyes of thousands of good people I am but as a poor outcast child of perdition—worse than a pagan."

"You are a real divine angel," exclaimed the young man; "Mrs. Osborne would love you—she must and shall know you," cried he, for at that moment every-thing seemed easy to him. "When they know you they will not oppose our union. I will steadfastly stick to business; my uncle is not a poor man; he will, I am sure, give me a share in his business. I will work so hard for you, and we will be so happy. I shall become good through you; I shall owe my salvation to you!"

"Amen!" said Jessie, solemnly; "but I, that am wiser than you in some things, must guide you a little. You are yet an apprentice—I am yet under my father's control: a time will come when we shall both be free. If you love me truly, you must wait till then. Five years from now shall be our time of trial. This is Christmas-day. You shall hear from me on the fifth anniversary of this day, but to me you shall not write. Five years from this time our trial shall have ended. Can you be true to me for so long?—I know that I shall be true to you!"

Lovers' vows sound foolish; therefore, we will not write down the violent protestations with which Williams responded to this singular proposal. He swore that neither heaven nor earth could ever change him—and at the time he thought so.

(For my part, I, that narrate this story, must here put in, by way of parenthesis, that had I been present, or had been in any way consulted, I should have said that such a connection was of that doubtful character, that, spite of Jessie's really superior nature, the best thing would have been to have put an end to the whole affair as soon as possible. But, as neither I nor anybody else of great discretion was present, the lovers made this compact, and then, the rest of the party joining them soon afterwards, they all adjourned to the village inn to dinner.)

It was as merry a dinner as ever was eaten by a set of poor players. They ate, and drank, and sung, and told witty anecdotes, and were ten times freer and easier than so many lords and ladies. The host and the hostess came to the parlour door, and listened and laughed too, and, spite of the really serious conversation which had passed between him and Jessie in the garden, Williams caught the infection of the company's mirth, and was as gay as any of them. Something was said of Mr. Goodman, and Williams, who had always maintained that he had some talent for acting, began to mimic his grave and measured way of speaking. His personation was called for again and again, and he was declared quite a genius. Bassett, they said, could not do it half as well. They then revealed to him a secret. Anderson, who had the talent for writing little comic pieces of one or two acts, had written one called " The Parson in Love," intended to ridicule Mr. Goodman : there was a young actress in the piece, Lucinda, who was to personate a puritan lady, Mrs. Tabitha Twiggem, who was to inveigle the clergyman, and lead him into endless fooleries. Jessie was to take this character and Bassett was to take that of Parson Perfect—and it was to be given out that he was a new actor from

London. Now Williams was so superior to Bassett that if he would only consent to take the character and act, they would manage it ;—they would put off Bassett with something else, or let him act in another piece,—but Williams must be their Parson Perfect ; —they would have no nay. Anderson, who was of the party, had a scene in his pocket, Williams must look it over and try it—he did so—Bravo ! bravissimo ! they exclaimed : it was inimitable ! Parson Goodman would never show his face after the public had seen that ; he would have had enough of preaching against players ! Williams, delighted to excel Bassett in anything, consented to act. Jessie heard all that went on, and did not oppose his acting. It was very clever, she said, and much better than she expected.

And now the company rose and began to talk of their departure. It was already dusk, and bitterly cold.

" Ah, my good fellow," said Anderson, who was deputed to be paymaster-general for the players, as he saw Williams about to put his hand in his pocket for his own share of the expenses—" have you a few spare shillings in your pocket, for the fellow has made me a deuced great bill—let me see, have you five-and-twenty ? "

Williams, who was in high good humour, and greatly flattered by the applause which his acting had obtained, drew out from his pocket a handful of loose change.

" Ah ! capital !" said Anderson, and took somewhere about seven-and-twenty shillings, saying, " we 'll have a reckoning when we get home."

Away drove the company. The snow, which had thawed in the morning, had frozen again in the afternoon, and it was terribly slippery, as well as cold. The gigs drove off, agreeing, on account of the bad state of the roads, to keep in company. Williams and Jessie were last. Perhaps Williams might be the worst driver in the company; perhaps, and most probably, his horse was the worst conditioned; however that might be, within the first two miles their companions got far ahead of them, and with every mile their horse seemed to become stiffer and clumsier; at last, down he came, but, fortunately not lower than his knees. Williams pulled him up again, and giving him a series of cuts with his whip, broke that useful instrument, but fortunately sent on his steed, for a short time, at least, at a much brisker and therefore safer pace. Everybody knows what a hopeless thing it is to drive a dull worn-out horse with a broken whip; slower and slower went the creature, and Williams pommelled with the stump of his whip, and flapped with his reins till he made himself quite hot.

"Ah! if our path through life should be like this," sighed poor Jessie; and scarcely had she finished the sentence when down came the horse flat to his nose, with his legs doubled under him. Crash! went one shaft, and out flew Williams on one side and poor Jessie on the other. It was a miracle that they were not both killed or had some bones broken. Williams sprang to his feet, hardly knowing that he was down, and with very becoming lover-like anxiety flew to look after his lady. Fortunately she was not hurt, not the least in the world, said she eagerly, in her turn inquiring after him. No, they were not either of them hurt—only Jessie then confessed to a very little pain in her wrist; she thought that she must have sprained it. Williams was in the greatest distress—what was to be done? For her, nothing, she said. There was a village just at hand, and thither she would hasten for help, whilst he stayed with the horse; and off she went, firm-footed as a young roe. The village was just by, and the most ready help was obtained at the first house. Men returned with her, with rope and lanterns, and presently the horse was on his legs again, not looking much worse than before, excepting for his broken knees; the shaft was tied together, and they were assured that there would be no difficulty about going forward, as the road was well tracked beyond the village, besides which, a peasant offered, for half-a-crown, to accompany them to the town with a lantern.

Very little was said by the lovers during the remainder of their journey. Jessie seemed sunk in thought, and so was Williams, for he was really frightened to think how he should get off with Evans, regarding the broken shaft and the broken knees of the horse. Money, he knew, would make all straight; but where in the world was the money to come from? He did not believe that he had more than a guinea left; thirteen shillings he had to pay for the hire of the horse and gig, and half-a-crown must go to the man with the lantern.

How those anxieties about money thrust themselves like evil demons between us and our pleasures—nay, even between us and our comforts! We have known many a dinner spoiled by the thought of the cost; many a good night's rest broken because some dire thought or other about want of cash has been gnawing at our heart! And thus it was with Williams; all the day's pleasure was spoiled to him now by the thought of the reckoning. At length the unfortunate steed stopped at the gate which led to his stable. It was not so late after all; it was only eight o'clock. Their companions had arrived long before and were all dispersed; but the first person whom Williams saw on dismounting was no other than Reynolds, who, on his side, stared in amazement, and then looked reproachfully. He had then been with that young actress to Alton! This was what he wanted the holiday for!

Without, however, waiting for a word from him, Williams called him aside, and putting the guinea into his hand, said, " Just run over, there's a good fellow, to Reeves's"—this was a small druggist and grocer's shop opposite, which Mr. Osborne supplied— " and get me change," for Williams knew that if he offered the full sum to Evans he should get no change, and change he must have to dismiss the peasant.

Reynolds, amazed as he was, yet thinking no harm, for he had always seen Williams with plenty of money, brought back the change.

" And now stop one moment with Miss Bannerman," said he, " whilst I get the fellow paid," for Williams preferred doing this alone. Reynolds, though full of prejudices against players, both male and female, could not refuse, and Williams soon after joined them, when both young men having accompanied Jessie to the patten-maker's door, went home together, but not before Williams had prescribed bandages and fomentations for the sprained wrist, and had promised to bring her that very night an embrocation himself.

If Williams had before been unfit to attend to his business, he was much more so now. Jessie was never out of his thoughts; considering that his aunt and uncle as it were espoused the cause of the players, he was for ever scheming whether he could not bring Jessie and his aunt acquainted; he thought of her being adopted as a daughter into the family—he thought of a thousand unlikely things—in fact, in the excited state of mind he then was, he could not tell probable from improbable things; not at all! He even thought of getting the two guineas which Evans demanded for the damaged horse and gig from poor Reynolds. Reynolds could borrow the money from his aunts as if on his own account, he thought.

Thus pondered and thus schemed Williams, and in the mean time his friends the players were preparing to bring out the new comedy of " The Parson in Love ;" the character of Parson Perfect to be performed by " a new actor from London," and the double character of Lucinda and TabithaTwiggcin by Miss Jessie Bannerman.

Williams duly received his part in MS., which he privately learned and rehearsed, not daring, for the life of him, however, to take Reynolds into his confidence on this subject, for ever since the night of the Fair Quaker of Deal he had been as vehement against players and playgoers as his aunts or Mr. Goodman himself.

A rehearsal of the whole piece was proposed at Mr. Maxwell's lodgings on Sunday afternoon, and thither of course Williams was summoned. But when he got there something very peculiar presented itself. There was Tom Bassett, to whom also a copy of the part of Parson Perfect had been sent— there he was, come to rehearse his part, and had brought with him an order for five-and-twenty tickets. How was this? both young men seemed to inquire—but there was nobody to answer them—the whole theatrical staff seemed to be in the next room, which was Mr. Maxwell's bed-room. Voices were heard in this said bed-room, loud voices and angry voices, too, and now and then the two rival amateur-actors had the pleasure of hearing their own names mentioned.

To pass away the awkward time, and to seem at his ease, Williams threw himself into an arm-chair and drew his manuscript from his pocket, and began to turn it over. Bassett seeing this, and instantly detecting that his rival's part actually was his own, pulled out his also, and seating himself opposite, glanced from the paper in his hand at his rival, with no very amicable expression of countenance. Just as Williams was about to return the expression the door opened, and in walked Jessie. She bowed courteously to both young men, and thus addressed them :—

" There has been a strange and almost ludicrous mistake made with regard to the part of Parson Perfect. Mr. Anderson, it seems, intended it for Mr. Williams."

" He himself offered it to me, my dear Miss Bannerman," interrupted Bassett.

Jessie waved her hand, and continued, " Mr. Anderson says that it was his wish that Mr. Williams should take the character. Mr. Maxwell on the contrary very much prefers Mr. Bassett having it. Very warm words," said she, smiling, " as no doubt you have heard—for the walls are thin—have arisen on the subject. This, however, is their decision, that I, who take the part of Lucinda, shall make the choice between you. Will you, gentlemen, give me your hands to be satisfied with my decision, and not let ill-will arise between you in consequence, for to one I must show a preference?"

" We will be quite satisfied," said they both, each sure of the preference, and took the offered hand, which was extended with the sweetest of smiles.

" Then, Mr. Bassett," said she, " you take the part. You are Parson Perfect and I Lucinda."

Williams dashed his manuscript to the floor and looked daggers at them both.

CHAPTER VII.

THE BUBBLE BURST.

THE next day the walls were placarded; the new comedy of The Parson in Love was to be acted with new scenery, new actors, and endless new attractions. The sight was gall and wormwood to Williams. He had nevertheless in the bottom of his soul the conviction that Jessie's decision was influenced by some feeling of advantage or propriety as regarded himself, but still he was mortified. In the eyes of his rival he was rejected.

The whole town talked of the new piece; a rumour got abroad that Mr. Goodman was to be quizzed. Some of the young actors' pranks in the town had caused a little scandal; the public mind was inclining against them. Good, sober house-keepers found their servants' heads turned about the theatre; housemaids read plays while they should have made beds; cooks gossiped for whole hours at the bakehouse about the handsome actors and actresses. Everything was evidently going wrong.

" It is high time those people left the town," said those who were just beginning to veer to the clergyman's side.

" Those disreputable people ought to be packed off by authority," said they who had thought with the clergyman all the time ; " and if they venture to ridicule him in their obscene plays, they *shall* be packed off—and that handily."

Williams had told Jessie that he would not go to the theatre that night ; that he could not bear to see her acting with Bassett. It would drive him mad, he said. Jessie did not urge it, and he was almost out of his mind with jealousy and chagrin. It is possible, however, that, after all, he might have gone, had it not been for an awkward affair which just then happened.

Mr. Osborne and Mr. Isaacs were together in the shop, when Mr. Reeves came in, and scratching his head, said, " Is young Reynolds anywhere about ?"

He was not, said Mr. Isaacs, he was gone into the country on business.

" Why, you see," said Reeves, addressing Mr. Isaacs, and leaning on the counter with both his elbows, and taking a guinea from his pocket—" that young gentleman got me to give him change, maybe a fortnight ago—on the evening of Christmas-day. Now it is an awkward thing to come with money so long afterwards—but I put the guinea aside at the time—I'll swear to it that it's the same—and now you see it's light weight. But young Mr. Reynolds will know all about it in a minute."

Long before this speech was ended, Mr. Osborne, who had come round the counter, took the guinea out of Reeves's hand and carefully examined it.

.He then went to his money-safe, and looking among his gold came back and asked Isaacs in an under-tone from whom he had the guinea?

" From Reynolds," returned Isaacs, and went on industriously polishing a pair of scales.

Williams came in at that moment, but Reeves was so often there on business that he took no notice, and seating himself at the apprentices' desk began to think of Jessie and the play.

" We will have it made right, Mr. Reeves," said Mr. Osborne hurriedly, when Williams came in. " Mr. Isaacs shall see you to-morrow."

When Reynolds returned in the evening he was summoned to Mr. Osborne's presence, who, producing the guinea, asked, " Do you know anything of this guinea ? "

Reynolds took it into his hand, and examining it, returned it, saying that he did not.

" Did you," inquired his master, " get change some little time ago from Mr. Reeves for a guinea?"

Reynolds changed colour slightly, and after a moment's pause, said, " I did."

" And whence had you the guinea ? " asked he.

Reynolds looked confused and was silent.

" There is something singular in this," said Mr. Osborne, " I must have an answer. The money was in my possession a little time ago. I knew it to be light, and marked it with a penknife that I might not pay it away. It has gone from my cash-box. I may have paid it away by mistake— but then how came it into your hands, or why do you refuse to account for it? I would not willingly suspect."

" Sir," interrupted Reynolds, " I am innocent of

what you suspect—I never took a sixpence which was not my own—but yet of that money I cannot give an account."

" It looks suspicious," said Mr. Osborne.

" It does," said Reynolds, " but that I cannot help—all I can ask is four-and-twenty hours for consideration."

" You shall have it," said Mr. Osborne.

It was Mr. Isaacs's custom after seven o'clock to sit in the back parlour, where he read the newspaper, or dozed a little,—after that time the apprentices were alone.

" Williams," said Reynolds, as soon as he was gone, " you have got me into a pretty scrape about changing that guinea for you."

Williams felt as if his very heart grew chill.

" It was light weight," said Reynolds, " and Reeves has brought it back again. Mr. Osborne insists on knowing how I came by it; there was, it seems, his private mark on it."

" How came he to know anything about it? ' asked Williams angrily. Reynolds told.

" The deuce take it !" muttered Williams.

" Well," said Reynolds, " it is your own affair, you know. I have confessed nothing, because I would not betray you—but if blame there be about it—you must bear it. I am innocent and can clear myself in a minute, and would have done so if it had not been for getting you into trouble about that girl."

" The deuce take it," again muttered Williams.

" You must make up your mind about what you'll do," said Reynolds, " I shall clear myself to-morrow."

" Clear yourself, and be hanged to you," returned

Williams—"clearing one's-self is easy enough—what, do you take me for a thief? It's easy enough to clear myself about the money—I don't look at every guinea that is given me—I received only the other day some money from Mrs. Osborne!—What a fuss is here about the money!—but the point is not to let it come out about taking Miss Bannerman to Alton. And then there is that wretched Evans dunning about his old dog-tit of a horse and his tumble-down gig—I was a fool for ever going to him! The fellow is as importunate as death. Now, I say, Reynolds, cannot you borrow the money for me? Won't your aunts or somebody lend it you?"

" You owe me already two pounds fifteen," said Reynolds,—" and as to borrowing from my aunts I do not believe that they will lend me any."

" Oh, for heaven's sake, go and try!" said Williams, deeply excited—" this shall be the last time that I ever will borrow from you. I 'll turn over a new leaf, I do assure you I will! I 'll be as steady as you are!"

We need not go through all the conversation that ensued, the flatteries, the entreaties, the confessions of past folly and extravagance, and the humble, contrite promises of amendment, all of which so worked upon Reynolds that he consented to make one more attack on his aunts.

When he reached his aunts, he found them in a state of vast excitement. Mrs. Proctor, the great town gossip, had just been there, and had brought a long exaggerated history of how the heads of all the apprentices in the town were turned with the players, and how, in particular, both of Mr. Osborne's young men were in love with one of them; they had been seen walking late at night with that good-for-nothing Bannerman ; they had hired gigs for her and driven about the country with her, and spent money upon her without 'end.—There was a bunch of flowers that somebody had given her—no doubt one of them —which cost fifteen shillings, and which Mary Parker, the butter-buyer, had brought by order from a gardener's in Birmingham. It was a sin and a shame that they were allowed to remain in the town, for thus these young men might be led into practices that might ruin them for life.

As he entered he found his aunt Joanna with her bonnet and cloak on, and with her servant dressed also, and with a lantern in her hand. Joanna, late as it was, full of zeal for the good name of her nephew, was setting out to Evans's, to make him recall his words with regard to her nephew taking out the players in gigs. She knew, she said, that Evans was wrong, and those who were to blame should bear the blame, and not the innocent. It was in vain that Reynolds made light of the matter as regarded himself ; she was bent upon vindicating him, and he, half in anger and half with miserable apprehension for his friend, whose cause he felt as if he must espouse, sat down with his aunt Dorothy to wait the other's return.

On her return she came fraught with new tidings. It was Williams who had hired the gig ; he had taken a tribe of players with him to Alton, had treated them at the inn, where they had all got drunk, and in driving home like so many mad folks Williams had thrown down his horse, ruined it for ever, and broken the gig into the bargain.

"This comes," said Miss Kendrick, " of Mr.

Osborne's encouraging those abandoned people; considering what might be the natural and inherited impulses of Williams, Mr. Osborne ought to have been doubly on his guard. But he has sown in the whirlwind and he may reap in the storm," said Joanna with emphasis.

Reynolds fired up at once. " It was not generous to be ripping up poor Williams's family misfortunes —what would she say if people did so by him ; he never would stand by silently and hear his friend thus spoken of."

It was a luckless rencontre. There was always a something in what the one said to excite the other. Poor Dorothy tried to make peace between them, but did not succeed. However, the end of it was that Reynolds must stay supper with them, and then, grown quite bold and desperate, he asked his aunts to lend him two guineas.

Joanna actually started ; " here was more of the devil's work," she said, adopting for the first time the clergyman's phrase—" no, she would not lend him a sixpence."

" I will," said Dorothy, " not that I am satisfied of all being right. But if he have done wrong we will hope that he may do so no more. We must endeavour to rule by love and not by severity, Joanna."

Reynolds returned home with the money.

There was not a deal of sleeping at the Osbornes' that night. Mr. and Mrs. Osborne talked over, with the deepest sorrow, the sad discovery which they believed was about to be made regarding Reynolds ; he who had seemed so steady, so, almost religious—how they grieved for his poor aunts. All the little pique was forgotten. Mrs. Osborne felt as if, from this time forth, she should show them nothing but kindness, for this was indeed a sore grief that would cut them up sadly. " Poor Miss Kendricks !" that was the beginning and the end of their consultations.

Very little sleep, too, was there in the apprentices' room ; none at all in Williams's bed. Now he thought of throwing himself at his aunt and uncle's feet, and confessing his love for Jessie and begging them to see and to hear her—if he could not move them, he was sure she could ! Now he thought of confessing to having taken the money, and leaving Jessie to stand or fall, trusting to the future as regarded her ; for their own credit's sake, he believed that they would shield him from public disgrace ; then he tried how it would be if he steadfastly declared the light guinea to have been given him by Mrs. Osborne —but then came the difficulty about its being changed at Reeves's. It was a bad, entangled affair, and he vowed with himself, that once clear of it, and all his little debts paid, he never would get into any such mess again !

The next morning he was up early, and set out to pay Evans and have done with him. Unfortunately, however, he went a little out of his way that he might pass the patten-maker's, and thus have the pleasure of passing the house that held Jessie. A slight tap at the parlour-window arrested his steps. It was old Mrs. Bellamy, who in her old night-cap stood there, and beckoned him in. Jessie was down also, and, early as it was, they were going to breakfast.

" We shall not now remain many days here," said Jessie on his entrance, " if, indeed, many hours. You are angry with me I know, but you will presently see that it was the truest regard for you which influenced my decision. This wretched pasquinade was not my doing; and when you hear those who are really good and excellent in the town—among the rest the Osbornes—censuring me for my part in it, then, remember, I was but as the puppet; others pulled the wires; had I been a free agent it should not have been so. But Edward," said she solemnly, " if you hear the worst and the most unjust things said against me, do not bring yourself into trouble by defending me. You know me better than they, and that is enough."

" You shall not go with these people!" said Williams. "Oh, if Mrs. Osborne did but know you!"

" It is impossible," returned Jessie, " she, like everybody else, will take against me. You will hear how we shall be abused; it will be a disgrace to have been acquainted with us. All I ask, then, is, that in your own heart you will not disown me. Never mention my name—but oh, Edward!" said she, with tears in her eyes—" if young men ever have serious moments of prayer—then remember me."

The young man made the most passionate vows of fidelity.

" And now," said she, " we part—you must not attempt to see me again. We shall meet again—but not yet—in five years—and then, perhaps, not to part again.—Till then, farewell!"

There was something so singular and solemn in her manner, that Williams felt almost awed. He seemed to himself to stand like a block, and do nothing—what was vowing fidelity—he must give her some token of his truth. He had not a ring to break between them, but he had a guinea—he rushed out to the patten-maker's shop and cut a guinea in two. " Here is gold broken between us," said he, " keep ône half for my sake ! "

" It is *cut*, not broken," said the old woman, " and that is unlucky.'

"Money," said Jessie, " was not needed between us—what nonsense it was to do so—a lock of your hair would have been better—or, best of all, nothing —for true-love needs no token—yet I will not refuse your gift," said she, putting the gold into her bosom. —Now farewell—and when I am evil spoken of—do not let your heart be ashamed of me ! "

" Never," said Williams; " the worse they say the better shall I love you ! "

No sooner was Williams out of the house than he thought how foolishly he had done in sacrificing the guinea ! How much wiser she was than himself ! He could not now pay Evans, and there was nothing to do but go home to breakfast.

"It never rains but it pours," says one proverb ; and another, which means the same thing, says that " misfortunes never come alone." It was so now with poor Williams. ·But before he reached home we must mention what he saw as he left the patten-maker's door. A group of men and boys were tearing down from the walls the players' bills, and daubing those which they could not reach, with mud. It was as Jessie had said ; public abhorrence had set in against the players.

When Williams arrived at home, who should be standing in the shop but Evans ; fortunately Reynolds alone was there.

" Oh," said Williams, without allowing Evans time to speak, " I have been in search of you—there's a guinea for you. What do you come after me for ? "

" After you," said Evans; looking at the guinea

with disdain, " why am I to be overhauled,—I was
by Miss Kendrick last night, as an abettor of players
and the very scum of the earth; why? I say, and I'll
ask it of any man! "

" Ask who you will," returned Williams in an
agitated voice, " but, for Heaven's sake, begone with
you. You know that I mean to pay you honestly.—
I set out this morning to pay you.—Now, for
Heaven's sake, I would not that Mr. Osborne knew
anything about it! "

" Will you pay me or not?" asked Evans doggedly,
holding out his hand with the one guinea in it.

"Are you indebted two guineas to this man for
mischief done to a horse and gig hired by you to take
a player to Alton on Christmas-day?" asked Mr.
Osborne in an awful voice close behind him.

He saw that he was betrayed, and turning pale as
death he said not a word.

Evans, who really was not a bad-hearted man, was
sorry in a moment for what he had done, and began
to apologise—he could wait—he was sorry, only he
had been provoked, &c.

It was too late either to be sorry or to apologise.
Mr. Osborne again sternly demanded from his nephew
if the money were due—if he had promised to pay it.

" He makes that demand," said Williams, " but
the horse was broken-knee'd and broken-winded—"

Mr. Osborne cut his explanation short by putting
another guinea into Evans's hand and bidding him go
about his business.

With a sad countenance Mr. and Mrs. Osborne sat
down to breakfast. Everybody were drinking their
coffee in silence, when a loud knock at the private
door startled them all. The next moment the Rev.
Mr. Goodman entered; and Mr. Isaacs, who had not

made half a breakfast, rose from his chair, and went out. The two apprentices were about doing the same thing, when Mr. Goodman begged that they might stay. He seemed very much excited; he came, he said, to complain of the vile, obscene pasquinade, which had been acted the night before, and in which he heard with sorrow and the deepest astonishment that a character intended to ridicule himself had been performed by this young man, said he, pointing to Williams, and with this he drew from his pocket a play-bill, and pointed out, " Parson Perfect—a young amateur actor from London."

" You are under a mistake, my dear sir," said good Mr. Osborne, really glad to be able to defend his nephew.

" I think I may go," said Reynolds, anxious not to witness the trouble which he feared hung over his friend.

" You may not go," said the clergyman sternly. " I have promised your excellent aunts to question you. I thought well of you, Reynolds," said he mournfully—" it has cut me to the heart to be deceived in you ! "

" And what have I done ? " asked he.

" This impatience is unbecoming," said the clergyman, " very unbecoming ! Can you deny that you walked up and down the town, arm-in-arm, with that young girl, Bannerman, on Christmas-day-night ? "

As Reynolds was about to reply, Miss Kendrick walked in, and scarcely was she seated when in rushed Mrs. Proctor, regardless of times and seasons. She came with a budget of news; but nobody could listen to her, and she went out again with something more interesting than all the rest to spread abroad, and that was of the awful conclave that was sitting in Mr. Osborne's parlour.

PART II.

CHAPTER I.

OLD ACQUAINTANCE AND NEW.

Mrs. Proctor and her favourite friend and gossip, Mrs. Morley, who now, after an absence of some years, had returned to reside again in the town, were sitting together at tea. The little white muslin blind was taken down from the window, for they wanted to have a good view of a funeral that was about to take place. Mrs. Proctor fortunately lived just by the church, so that she consequently saw all the marriages and funerals, and mostly invited some of her friends to see them with her. The funeral-bell now tolled solemnly; the sun shone calmly over the beautiful church-yard, and on the open grave, and on the slow procession that now advanced towards it. The ladies at their window made their remarks; "it was a very handsome funeral; the very first people of the town at it, and no wonder, for Mr. Osborne was respected by everybody.—And there was young Williams, whom the Osbornes had adopted as their son—what a handsome young man he was, and how well he looked in his mourning!"

Thus they made their comments and then sat down to talk.

"Well, I've heard say," said Mrs. Proctor, "that young Williams is as a relation of theirs—some suppose a son of that poor Phebe Phillips, Mrs. Osborne's sister, that married so badly—but I don't know—it may or it may not—however, you see, they were always very fond of him, and behaved to him as if he were their own son. When there was all that stir and scandal about the players! Lord, what a stir it made! They took his part and cleared him through thick and thin—though folks said there was something very scandalous and shameful, if it could only have come out. Nobody knew justly what it was, but those Miss Kendricks, who after that time were ten times more intimate than ever,—and Mr. Goodman, who was vicar here at that time. Well, as I was saying, after all that scandal, poor Mrs. Osborne never rightly was herself again. She had no regular complaint, but she got ailing; now she went here and now there—now for change of air, now for mineral waters, and now for sea-bathing. It was well for Mr. Osborne that he had such a trustworthy person in his shop as Mr. Isaacs—young Reynolds was out of his time and was gone—was gone to some great house in London—his aunts thought of making something out of the common way of him—and it was well I say that Mr. Osborne had that steady Mr. Isaacs with him, for after his wife was so poorly he never rightly cared about business—there ain't many such husbands!"

"I've heard say," remarked Mrs. Morley, "that it was a love-match at first."

"Like enough," returned her friend, "and old

folks as they were, they were like lovers to the last.
Folks said," continued she, " that all the trouble he
had with his apprentices made him sick of business,
and so he made Isaacs a sort of partner, and turned all
management over to him. Young Williams was gone
too—and then after three or four years they sent for
Reynolds again—old Isaacs couldn't do without him
—and when he came, Lord, what changes he brought
with him—he'd got new notions in London—must
have the old shop-front out—puts up new windows.
—Inside and outside all was changed—begins some
sort of manufacturing—gets head-man at once—
Williams then comes back too—a fine young man
indeed is he!—puts on a shop-apron again and buckles
to—but anybody could plainly see that it was only to
please the old folks. She died, however, and then
when she was gone the old man was a regular wreck—
broker-up in no time!—Why he was only sixty-
nine when he died!—"

" I've heard Nurse Gee say," remarked Mrs. Morley, " that it was quite cutting to hear him in his
dreams talking to her—and then when he woke and
found how it was—it was up with him for days.—He
got quite childish before he died.—I wonder how he
has left his property ? "

Some weeks after this the ladies were again
together, and with them Miss Jenkins, who was
cousin to Lawyer Bishop's wife, and she it was who
had first brought the news to her friends that Mr.
Osborne's will had surprised everybody—he had left
positively twenty thousand pounds, every penny of
which went to Williams, without a farthing's legacy
to go out of it. His house and business he left
jointly to old Isaacs, Reynolds, and young Williams,

only Williams's name was to stand first in the firm.

The ladies were again talking on this subject, which was not easily exhausted, when another was introduced in consequence of a small modest-looking card being brought in by Mrs. Proctor's maid, and which ran thus, "Marianne Jervis, Miniature-painter, and Teacher of Fancy Work of all kinds, at Mrs. Cope's, Milliner, Balance Street."

"Oh," said Miss Jenkins, recognising the card at first sight, "that is really a wonderful girl, have you seen none of her work? She does all kinds of work —paints miniatures delightfully — does poonah painting, and makes rice-paper flowers and wax flowers—just like life—and makes bags of bead-work; and paints screens; and does everything; and so cheap—it's wonderful!—You may find your own materials if you like; and she makes them up beautiful! Mrs. Tom Bevington has bought some wax flowers from her, and my cousin Mrs. Bishop is going to have her to paint the baby, and the black spaniel. She has Mrs. Cope's parlour: there is her father with her, a very old-looking man, who goes about with little packets of stationery, boxes of steel-pens, wafers and sealing-wax, wrapped up together, saying that, ' all these are for one shilling only:' he leaves them one day and calls for them the next; and looks like a broken-down gentleman."

"He has been here," said Mrs. Proctor, " but I make a principle of never encouraging beggars of any kind."

"They are not exactly beggars," said Miss Jenkins, who had established herself as a patroness of the young *artiste*—" and she is the loveliest little creature you ever saw, so small and delicately made; with a complexion like marble; and yet pretty as she is, she is so steady and so kind to her father, and works so hard—Mrs. Cope says she is always up till after midnight.—Have you never seen her?" asked she—neither of the ladies could recollect having done so—but how did she dress?

" Always in black," returned Miss Jenkins, " in a black stuff frock, little black cloak, and a close black chip bonnet."

No, the ladies had never seen her, nor had they much desire to see her. There was something mostly not quite right about such people. Many thought that Mrs. Cope, considering that she was now a widow, and had just begun business, ought to mind whom she took into her house. She got into a sad scrape some years ago, when her husband was living, with having some good-for-nothing players lodging there. They wished, for her sake, that it might all turn out right.

We will now, the friendly reader and myself, look into that same little parlour, which formerly we called the patten-maker's, but which for the last twelve months served the patten-maker's widow as her little show-room ; but which now she had let, business not being very successful, to the young miniature-painter and maker of fancy-work, and her dejected-looking father.

" And, father dear, don't be cast down," said the young girl, " I am sure that he would not have the heart purposely to avoid you. There must be some accident about the letter being returned ; depend upon it, one so young, and brought up with such good people, must be good like them. All will be right in time ; only, father dear, do not be cast down !" said she, throwing her arms round his neck, and playfully twisting her small fingers in his thin gray hair. " It has not been combed," said she, " all the morning;" and, taking a small case-comb from her father's waistcoat pocket, she began smoothing and arranging his hair. It seemed to have a soothing influence on him ; he sat still, and his face grew calmer.

" Well, well, child," said he at length, putting her gently from him, " I must be going, and if I am not back to-night, don't be alarmed. I shall go round by Lichfield and Burton, and may be absent two or three days."

" But I must know, first of all," said she, cheerfully, " that all is ready for your journey. Have you got your night-cap ? Nay, I must see it before I can believe. Ah, good, yes ! And your gloves ? and let me see that there are no holes in them. Sit down like a dear father, while I mend them ; you will have walking enough before you come back!" and, so saying, the dear, cheerful, little creature took out her little needle-book and thimble, and mended up the old gloves as tidily as if they had been new, though anybody but she would have said that they were past mending months ago. How like the most skilful of valets she brushed his old coat, which, like his gloves, had seen its best days long ago, chatting and singing all the while like a spirit of love and gladness as she was.

When all these little offices were done for him, and the neat little paper of sandwiches put into his pocket before his eye, and he duly warned to remember that he had them with him, and not to do as he did sometimes, go famishing all day, and then bring them home dry in his pocket at night—which she assured him was anything but economical.—When all this was done, and his blue camlet-bag, which looked very much like a lawyer's, and which contained his neat little packets of stationery, was set on the table before him, she brushed his hat, and set his stick ready for him; and then kissing him, woke him from a reverie into which he had fallen.

Poor man! he looked harassed and weary, and not fit to begin a foot-journey, even of two days · and so his daughter thought, and at another time she might have urged his staying at home, but now she had reasons of her own for wishing him out of the way, at least for a little while; so begging him always to keep the shady side of the road, and not to be afraid of spending sixpence or a shilling in getting an occasional lift in a returned chaise or even a cart, and never to walk too far without resting, she did her best to speed him on his way, and the poor day-dreaming, unfortunate man took up his bag and stick, and, kissing her tenderly, went out.

CHAPTER II.

A CONTRE-TEMPS.

As soon as her father was gone, she set herself busily to work; first of all, she took all her little store of fancy-work and painting out of the window, dusted the inside of the window, blew every particle of dust from the various articles, and thought to herself how fortunate it was that this window lay to the north, and thus had so little sun to fade the things, though it was a pity that even here the flies made such work over everything. But, however, all was now neatly arranged in the window, and she thought that they had never looked so nice before ; next she set out her little table with her drawing materials, and reared up the miniature of Mrs. Bishop's chubby baby, which was not at all amiss, and the large drawing of the black spaniel, and made everything look neat and business-like, that if Mrs. Cope had to bring anybody in during her absence, things might look to advantage.

All this ended, and nobody in this world could make poverty wear a fairer face than Marianne, she went into her little chamber to dress. She had her own reasons for wishing to look very charming this morning. She had often been to the smart new-fronted shop of Williams, Isaacs, and Co.; she had been sent there by her father for wafers and ingredients for his cheap sealing-wax; and old Mr. Isaacs and young Mr. Reynolds had taken great notice of her; Williams she had never seen. Some way or other young Reynolds always served her ; she liked to be served by him in preference to any one, and whenever she had been to the shop, he could never think of anything but her all day long, and many a night he had dreamed of her. She had done the very same thing by him. He talked of sitting for his miniature, and she wished with all her heart that he would.

Marianne knew her father's history, knew the reason for his coming to that town. It was the parable of the prodigal son reversed—it was the prodigal father seeking reconciliation with his fortunate son. He had sought for that reconciliation, and had been repulsed, disowned, treated as an impostor, and now his humble, touching letter had been returned unanswered. He was disheartened, wounded, crushed to the earth. He understood that his son passed much of his time at Burton; to Burton therefore he went, but without explaining his intention to his daughter, determined to have an interview, and to drag pity and justice from him. Marianne, knowing her father's unsuccess, doubted in her own mind if he had gone wisely to work. She could not conceive her brother to be the harsh, proud, cold-hearted being that her father had found him. Her father had forbidden her interfering, but now, however, she was resolved to make the attempt upon her own responsibility, and her good, hopeful heart said that she would succeed.

She was still dressed in the black stuff frock, little black cloak, and chip bonnet, but when she went tripping down stairs, and through Mrs. Cope's room, that good woman thought she had never seen her look so gay and lovely. "What in the world has the young creature in hand," said she, as she looked down the street after her, " she is a good angel, bless her little heart! that she is!"

Down the street went Marianne, and across the next, right up to the smart chemist's shop, where stood Reynolds, looking very gay and smart too, while two apprentices and old Mr. Isaacs were attending to customers. Reynolds, like Mrs. Cope, thought that he had never seen Marianne look so charming before, —there was a half-timid, half-trustful, and most peculiar expression, so good, so kind, yet so modest, in her face, as she looked at him, and asked for two-pennyworth of Indian rubber. He flew behind the counter, took out a drawer, picked out the very nicest pieces, all square and smooth, and every one of them sixpence a piece.

" Is this two-pence?" asked she, taking up the very largest and nicest.

" It is," said he.

She took two-pence from her little black silk bag, and wrapping them up in a small piece of writing paper, on which some words were written, gave them to him.

She saw him read the words—that was what she intended—and yet, for the life of her she could not help feeling almost faint as she did so; and without venturing another glance at him, she put the Indian rubber, which he had carefully wrapped up for her, in her bag, and hurried out paler than ever; and with such a trembling in her knees, that she thought certainly she should drop.

Reynolds, on his part, was no less agitated; the words on the paper were these : " I am deeply interested in the happiness of one dear to me as life; this obliges me to ask a private interview with you. Will you meet me this afternoon at four o'clock, in the fields between the old cotton mill and Crake-marsh."

Reynolds asked himself a thousand questions, not one of which he could answer. His feelings were of a very mixed kind. For one moment he was sorry that she had done this; the next he was charmed and flattered. What young man of five-and-twenty would not have been so too ?

At half-past three, he was sitting, very carefully dressed—he had never taken such pains with his person before—on the stile just beyond the old cotton mill, looking towards the town, that he might catch the first glimpse of her; and a little after he saw the light, neat, black-apparelled form of Marianne approaching. He leaped down from his seat, and sprang forward to meet her. She looked paler than ever, and greatly agitated. He would have taken her hand, but she withdrew it hastily, but not without his feeling how it trembled ; and standing still, she said gravely, "As yet all liberties with me are insults. Listen to me before you touch my hand, for as yet I appear to you but in a doubtful light. Fifteen years ago you parted with a little sister—do you remember her ?"

"I do," said the young man, striking his hand upon his forehead, " I remember her well."

"I, then, am that sister ! "

"You!" exclaimed he, with a feeling of almost disappointment. " You that little Susan whom I loved so much ! "

"If I were then called Susan," said she, " I have since then been called Marianne—there was much in that time to be forgotten."

"There was ! there was !" said Reynolds, " but we will not think of it now. We will forget all the past just now ; some other time you shall tell me all, we will rejoice now in the present," said he, taking her now unresisting hand, and putting it within his.

"And you will see our poor father, then," said she, " and acknowledge him ? "

He started, stopped short, and looked at her almost in horror.

"It is so, then ! " she said reproachfully, "you refuse to acknowledge him ! "

"How can this be?" said he, "is our father living? I thought that they had taken his life."

"No, thank God ! " she returned, " he was transported ; but," she said, imagining that now she saw why her father had been treated as an impostor by his son, "they never told you how it was really. I daresay he was but seldom spoken of."

"Never!" said Reynolds, "I never heard them speak of him; my feelings have always been so much considered. And he lives then, actually?"

"Yes, lives," said she, "and is so changed that even you—that nobody—need be ashamed of him—poor as he is. But he is so good, so gentle, his only fault is that he loves me too well, has adventured too much for me. Oh, how thankful I am that you will own him! I always thought you would. Often have I come to the shop, just to see you—you looked to me so good and amiable," said she, blushing, and looking affectionately in his face.

"I declare I never saw anybody's bonnet fit their heads so prettily as yours," exclaimed he, stopping suddenly, and letting go her arm. "Come, I must see this bonnet off," said he, suddenly untying the strings—"No, I won't crush the dear little bonnet, not I. I tell you what, you ought never to wear a bonnet; it's a sin and a shame to hide your head."

"Oh, give me my bonnet," said she, "you make me quite ashamed!"

"I shall not give up the bonnet till I have had a kiss," said he; and without further ceremony caught her in his arms, and kissed her forehead and lips.

"I tell you what," said he, "I really am sorry, after all, that you are my sister. I would a deal rather have had you for my wife."

"I'll come and keep your house for you," said she, "that I will; you have no notion what a good house-keeper I am."

"No, you shall not keep my house," said he, "else I know somebody that will be falling in love with you, and then you will never care a jot for me. No, I shall put you under a glass case, and keep you all to myself."

Thus talked he; and Marianne, happier than ever she had been before in her life, walked by his side, addressing him as "William" and "brother" most affectionately, and thinking that she could not have patience to wait till her father's return. At length, in the midst of her happiness, one thought of regret came to her mind, and she said, " It was a great disappointment to my poor father to find my aunt dead. He hoped with her to find me a home."

Again Reynolds stopped. "Dead!" repeated he. "She is not dead. She is alive and well, and will love you dearly, that she will; and so will poor Aunt Dorothy. Come, we will go there at once—how I shall surprise them! Aunt Dorothy shall lay her hand on your head, and feel your face, and then she will know how lovely you are."

"Aunt Dorothy?" asked Marianne, "of her I never heard.'

" I daresay you never did," said he. "She is blind, poor thing, and thus is not as active as her sister; but she is as good. You will love her dearly."

"Now I shall go right through the town," said he, " with you leaning on my arm, and only be sorry that I cannot tell everybody I meet that you are my sister." And so he would have done, had he met anybody whom he knew; but it was one of those days when one chances to meet nobody, when nobody seems to be out: so he reached his aunts' door without remark or interruption.

"Now I shall astonish the old ladies," said he, rushing in. " Guess what I have brought you," said he, leaving Marianne in the outer room. The old ladies were very indulgent to their nephew; they guessed all kinds of things, but could not come near the truth. At length he went out, and returned with Marianne, saying, " My dear aunts, I introduce to you your niece."

It was a most complete shock—they thought that he was married, and that this was his wife. " Your wife?" asked they.

" No," returned he, "not my wife, I wish it were, but my sister, that sweet little sister Susan of whom I used to talk so much. Is she not sweet and charming, and does she not look good and loveable?"

" Sit down, sit down, my dear," said Joanna, who, though taken so by surprise, could not help seeing how confused and agitated the poor girl seemed.

Reynolds, who was quite vehement in his delight, would not, however, let her sit down till she had taken off her cloak and bonnet, that they might see," he said, " what a sweet little sister she was."

Poor Marianne, more confused now than ever, took the seat which Joanna offered to her. She was more confused and agitated every moment. That Reynolds was her brother she had never doubted for a moment; but this surely was not the aunt which she had heard described by her mother. This aunt had never been married surely! she wore no wedding-ring. The most fearful misgivings came over her mind; she felt almost faint with apprehension. " And where then is Mrs. Osborne?" asked she with anxious fear.

" My dear," said Joanna, " Mrs. Osborne has been dead these four years."

" She was my aunt! I have made some strange, some frightful mistake," said she, rising, and almost

bursting into tears. " Tell me," she said, addressing
Reynolds, "were you not born with the name of
Edwards, whatever you may now be called ? "

" This is the daughter of poor Mrs. Edwards,"
whispered Joanna to her sister, who, though blind,
took the most lively interest in what went forward.

Reynolds made no reply—a strange light burst in
upon his mind also, and a reality of happiness filled
his heart—but at that moment he could not have
expressed it.

" Oh, I have made some great, some frightful mistake !" again exclaimed the poor girl, looking round
her.

Joanna ran, and taking her hand, said with a look
of infinite kindness, " No, my dear, you have made
no great mistake after all; you are right in one
respect—you are among kind friends; we were friends
of your mother's—friends of your aunt's—we will be
friends also to you."

These words were meant to be consolatory. Marianne felt that they were spoken in the very spirit of
kindness, but the presence of the young man troubled
her beyond words ; she feared to ask who he was,
and how it was possible that this mistake could have
been made between them ; she dared not lift up her
eyes to him. He too was bewildered in his turn—
this, then, was not his sister, but Williams's; she had
mistaken him for Williams. The truth filled him
with rapture ; his heart from the first had told him
that he wished in her something dearer than a sister.
He almost shrunk back at the thought of the fami-
liarity which he had used towards her. He saw how
she felt too ; they stood in a very painful and embar-
rassing relationship to each other. He rose, and not

venturing even a glance at her, said that he would leave the young lady with his aunts. A cup of their excellent tea would do her good. In the evening he would return.

The quiet kindness of those amiable sisters, on whose every action sincerity was stamped, reassured the poor girl. They asked her no questions regarding herself, but talked of the bright young days of her mother, when they three had been happy, thoughtless girls together. They spoke of her aunt and uncle Osborne, as her mother had done; and when she asked of her brother, they told her nothing but what was good of him. He had been the companion and friend of William Reynolds, their nephew, for these ten years or more. Their nephew was the best young man in the world—on this subject they never were tired of speaking—they did not know what an agony it was to the poor girl. At length, in the fulness of her heart, she told all that had passed between them —her frequent visits to the shop, her hope of surprising her father in making themselves known to him, and being acknowledged by him, (of his unsuccessful attempts she said nothing,) and, now, what had she done? claimed a wrong relation—made herself appear forward and ridiculous, and all the time he must have known how inapplicable every word she uttered was to him. Oh! why had he allowed her thus to commit herself—thus to betray her father's secret?

The sisters could enter into her feelings—and to show their confidence in her, as well as to excuse their nephew, they told her what hitherto they had told to none—that their nephew's early history and family connexions bore sufficient resemblance to those of her brother, to make the mistake which had occurred so easy at first. Thus they proved to her that they thought her worthy of their confidence. In return she gave them hers; she told of their life in Australia; of her mother's goodness and industry, and her father's hardships and sufferings; how his spirit was broken by his disgrace, and how home-sick he was for England. Her mother lived in a school, and by her services paid for the education of her daughter. She did more than that—she gave daily lessons in Sydney, where they lived, and saved money. Anxiety and excessive labour, however, at length preyed upon her health; she had some kind friends, and by them her death was made as easy as possible. She had no anxiety about her daughter, for many desired to befriend her: her wish, however, was that she should return to England; she left written instructions to her husband, with three hundred pounds for this purpose; she left her daughter as a legacy to her beloved Aunt Osborne. Four years after her death, the father's term of transportation expired. He yearned to be back in his native land, and, taking his daughter and the money, embarked in one of the first ships sailing for London.

"In England," said his daughter, "he flattered himself, that, broken-down though he was in spirit and constitution, he could begin a new career. On the voyage he spoke with the utmost impatience of re-union with his son, of whom he was very fond. His nature was softened, rather than hardened, by calamity; he often wept like a child. He loved her," she said, "dearly, and was the most indulgent of fathers, and had formed, she could not tell what extravagant notions of her prosperity in England. He talked of London almost as the nursery song does, as

if the streets were paved with gold, Scarcely, however, had they landed in England, when he returned
home to his lodgings almost on the verge of despair.

He was again a ruined man, almost pennyless.
How it happened she could not tell; she suspected
that he had fallen into the hands of designing gam-
blers who had robbed him of all. He was in despair;
his health gave way, and, at the suggestion of the
kind woman with whom they lodged, she began to
paint miniatures and make fancy-work. She worked
incessantly, and made a large stock of things, which
she sold at good prices to the bazaars and shops. A
fellow-lodger, who took a great fancy to her father,
and who supported himself by dealing in common
stationery, was then ill, and shortly after died, leaving
to her father his little stock in trade, and his recipes
for ink and sealing-wax. This and her fancy-work
and painting had since then supported them. As
soon as he was better in health, and had somewhat
recovered his spirits, they came down here, intending
to make themselves known to her mother's sister; she,
however, was dead. And, then, as to her brother—"
poor Marianne blushed deeply—"yes, indeed, what
a strange blunder she had made!"

Such was her narrative; and the two sisters, even
the blind one, were as much charmed with her as
their nephew had been. Pretty she was, beyond
words; and she was wise, and clever, and cheerful-
hearted, had had sorrow enough to have bowed her
down to the earth, and yet she was as gay as a bird:
the truth was, there was a well-spring of gladness in
her heart, and that was the spirit of love that never
wearied in well-doing. She was a very jewel of a
human being, and so neat and fairy-like withal, and

had such pretty turns and ways with her that were quite natural to her, and looked so arch and good-tempered, that it put one in humor with life and one's-self, only to look at her. She was a perfect mistress of the art of pleasing—it was born to her, and therefore it was so easy.

She stopped all night at the Miss Kendricks. Their little maid went to Mrs. Cope's to say so, and to bring her night-things ; and Reynolds never got home that night till the clock was on the stroke of one.

CHAPTER III.

AGAIN, OLD AND NEW ACQUAINTANCE.

We have not now seen anything of Williams for some time ; not, in fact, for seven years. Time goes on with such strange rapidity now-a-days! Seven years it is since we saw either him or Jessie Bannerman. We will, first of all, inquire after him, and know something of the workings of his mind, for, if we are not mistaken, he must in some things be changed, since we saw him last. We have long known his growing aversion to trade—there is nothing at all remarkable in that. But as concerns Jessie, we must make some inquiries. This, then, is what regards her.

When all that great affair of the players occurred, his acquaintance with Jessie came to the knowledge of the Osbornes, and the painful circumstances regarding their nephew that came to their knowledge with it, caused them to imagine the worst things of Jessie. It was in vain, when he had confessed his love-engagement, that he tried to place her character in its true light. They could not, and did not, believe what he said. They regarded her as the most

designing and artful of *intriguantes*, only the more
detestable because she had worn the mask of innocence
and virtue. Williams yielded to the storm against
her. The storm blew over; the sunshine of his good
relation's favour again fell upon him. The time of
his apprenticeship expired; he was sent into the
world to look about him, not to labour. Poor Mrs.
Osborne's health began to give way, however, and
then he was recalled; her husband had not a thought
for anything but her; they took their adopted son
with them, and went from place to place to regain,
if possible, her health. She grew only worse and
worse, and died, blessing her nephew for having given
up his inclinations to please her. In reality, however,
he had not given up his inclinations from any sense
of duty; he had only become indifferent about them
He had begun to look back to the days of his acquaintance with Jessie, and his jealousy of Tom
Bassett, as of days which it was as well to forget;
not but that certain uneasy qualms came over his
heart when he thought of the fair Jessie, and his
plighted faith to her. But sufficient for the day is
the evil thereof, thought he, and left it to care for
itself. The appointed day at length came—the fifth
anniversary of that strange Christmas-day at Alton,
and he had curiosity enough to inquire at the Post-
office if there were a letter for him. There was a
letter from Jessie, and it ran thus:—

"Punctually at the time fixed I now write. A
few words are enough. I will deal candidly with
you. Life has gone variously with me since we
parted. I have now nothing more valuable to offer
you than love and gratitude. Wealth, however, in
comparison of these treasures of life, is mere dust,

Are you ready and willing to fulfil your engagement?
I have been true to you. If there be a moment's
doubt on your mind, you are free.   J. B."

Such was her letter. Williams sat and pondered.
It troubled him; but then could he really marry,
and bring home as his wife, that girl against whom
so much had been said? No, he never could! besides,
what would his uncle say?—what would Mrs. Proctor,
what would everybody say? It was a very silly affair
altogether—a boyish folly. People could not live on
love and gratitude; if there were plenty of money,
it would be a different affair. No, no, he must put
an end to it at once.

He wrote. His letter might have served as a
model for the Complete Letter-Writer. He spoke
most feelingly of the death of his aunt, of his sense of
duty to her, of the force of circumstances, of his own
future and present dependence on his uncle, of the
sacrifice he had been compelled to make of his feelings, of his unworthiness of her, of the certainty
that she would meet with one much more deserving;
in short, the letter said, as plainly as letter could say,
that, to use a common phrase, he desired to wash his
hands of the whole thing.

He heard no more from her. She sent no letter
of reproach or remonstrance; and he began to
congratulate himself on having so well got rid of the
connection.

Not long after this, his uncle's death left him very
unexpectedly possessed of so handsome a legacy as
gave him quite another position in life. He began to
take ambitious views, but still he was man of the
world enough to bear his greatness with a very philo-

8

sophical calmness, and had it been twenty times the
sum, he would have done the same.   What infinite
folly seemed now all his connection with players and
all such low people!   It seemed to him a merciful
deliverance to have done with Jessie Bannerman.

He renewed his acquaintance with Tom Bassett,
who was now a prosperous lawyer, living on the
sunny side of life, in the pleasant little town of
Burton-on-Trent.   Tom was a very prosperous man,
and had just married the daughter of a rich country
gentleman.   A prosperous country banker too was
the elder brother, with a fine country-seat as well as
his house. in the county-town.   The Bassetts were
people with whom it was creditable to associate, and
with them Williams talked of investments and purchases.   He began to turn his mind to the buying of
a country-house.   Though his name was the first in
the firm, and stood in great gold letters over the
shop-door, he was very rarely now at the shop—came
now and then as a convenience—dined there and
slept there occasionally, but passed most of his
time in a lovely cottage ornée, which he had taken
furnished, by the month, near Burton.

Williams cultivated the Bassetts' acquaintance with
more zeal than they his.   All at once, however, the
lawyer became very zealous; it had occurred to him
that the family might make use of him on a particular occasion.   Williams talked often of buying a small
estate, with a good house upon it.   The Bassetts
had one to sell.   It had belonged to the late Mrs.
Bassett; it was the property of the daughter, who
now occupied it, but, finding it lonely during the
winter, she wished to leave it.   Her brothers advised
her to sell it, and invest the money in railroad shares,

which would pay much better interest. Williams
was just the purchaser they wanted, one who had
plenty of money, and wanted to lay some of it out.
They were charmed with the thought, and nothing
could exceed the lawyer's friendliness. The next
time Williams talked of investing some of his money
in the purchase of a small estate, Bassett suddenly ·
recollected that his sister might be induced to sell.
Nothing in the world could be more desirable than
her place, it was just what he wanted—in excellent ·
condition, neither too large nor too small, with just
the right quantity of land—a thorough gentleman's
place. Williams's wishes were excited; and then he
was informed that the sister was willing to sell; he
might see the place; he should take a note to her the
next day.

"He'll bite!" said Tom Bassett, chuckling to
himself, and thinking that he had managed it famously. A word, now, respecting the lady herself. She
was older than her brother, was in fact two-and-
thirty, a really good, excellent creature, who, if she
looked as old as she was, made you forget everything
but how good she was. She was spoken of in her
own neighbourhood as something quite uncommon.
She had a school for the poor children, which she
superintended herself every day; she visited the poor,
lent them good books, and befriended them in a
hundred ways; she was just the person calculated
for a country clergyman's wife. Her brother had a
husband in view for her, and desired nothing more
than to get her away from her cottage in Needwood
Forest, where, he said, she buried herself alive. He
wanted her to marry a man who was willing to marry
her, and who would have the means of putting busi-

ness in his brother-in-law's hands. She was a very strictly religious lady, too, and, some people said, had but little charity with the shortcomings of others— but they might be wrong, and we think they were.

The note of introduction which Williams brought from her brother, insured him quite a friendly reception; she ordered luncheon in for him, and then led him over her grounds, showed him her shrubbery-walks, and her rockery, and her grotto, and her summer-house, and her little pond with water-lilies, and her little greenhouse, and all her geraniums and her fuchsias and cape-heaths, and heaven knows what, growing in little heart-shaped beds, and standing on elegant green stages and rustic flower-stands; they sat down together on garden-seats side by side, and she pointed out views to him which he admired; they looked into the kitchen-garden, and talked about marrowfat peas, and the best mode of growing tomatoes; they peeped together into the melon-frame, and she gathered a melon which he carried into the house. It is astonishing how friendly they became in that short time. Then they came into the house, and he was taken into the nice little breakfast-room, where were her books; and the dining-room, and the little boudoir—it was too small for a drawing-room —where stood her harp, and her piano, and again her flowers; and there were pictures of herself smiling on the walls, here with her hair cut short, and in a prim white frock and pink sash, a demure little school-girl; and there at eighteen, fresh as a rosebud. Williams thought to himself what a wonder it was that she was not married at eighteen. After he had gone through the house, he went to take his leave of her, but he did not take his leave; they sat and talked; then he had forgotten some little particular about the garden-fence; he begged again to see it; the afternoon was charming—it was a long way to the end of the garden—he feared he might lose his way; it was very polite of her indeed—she put on her bonnet and shawl, and walked with him again. All along those winding walks they went, on grass as smooth as velvet, and passed first one flower-stand and then another, up by the rockery and pool of water-lilies, till they reached the very end of the garden—and there they sat down in the summer-house. Miss Bassett was older than her visitor; he was her brother's friend, so they felt quite at ease one with another, and the end of all this walking and talking was, that Williams, instead of negotiating about the purchase of the place, made her an offer of marriage—she had fifteen thousand pounds beside the place—he made her an offer of marriage, and was accepted.

He felt that he had done a good day's work—he never was so well satisfied with himself before. He mounted his horse, and rode home, not to his cottage at Burton, but to the shop. The side parlour, where in former days his uncle and aunt, good, quiet people, had passed their time, and received their friends, was now his own particular room. Nobody entered it without his permission, and there he transacted his private business: and there, as he sat that evening, in a large easy-chair, in the pride of his successful wooing, never dreaming of his father, came that father, for the first time, to claim his love and his compassion. Had Mr. Osborne risen from the dead to snatch from him his twenty thousand pounds of legacy, the shock could hardly have been greater than it was, when that man, who seemed to belong to

the class of genteel beggars, or broken-down tradesmen, stepped forward, and in words almost inarticulate
from emotion, said in a hollow voice, " William !
my son! I am your father!"

It might, or it might not, be so—the stranger bore
no resemblance to his father, as he remembered him;
but, at all events, the rencontre was unpleasant. He
assumed his coldest air ; he seemed to disbelieve ; he
refused to look at any documents which the stranger
produced; he said he had an engagement, looked at
his watch, and rose from his chair. The father, who
was much cut down, wept ; and the son, disturbed
and displeased, and yet troubled with the apprehension that it might be true, gave him two guineas, and
begged that he might not hear of him again; he
really could not thus be molested—it was extremely
unpleasant.

The poor man walked submissively away ; he felt
in the depths of his soul how hard it is for the poor
to take hold on the souls of the rich. Again and
again they met, and Williams, who, of all things,
saw how undesirable was such a claimant and such a
connection, shut his heart against conviction, and
doled out relief as if to a common importunate beggar.
The father grew angry, rose in his demands, talked
of an appeal to the magistrates to have his claim
on his son enforced: and the son, on his part, who,
. however, would have made any sacrifice rather than
that the thing should become public at all, threatened
to have the father prosecuted as an impostor.

During these hard contests between father and son,
the Bassett brothers heard, with the utmost amazement and vexation, of the engagement between their
sister and Williams. They were fairly taken in their

own net, and were only the more angry from that fact. Every argument now that could be advanced against Williams was brought forward—his being, as it were, *nobody*—his early connection with the players—his shop. But these arguments had no weight with the lady; she was not a child, she said, to be turned about by the first adverse opinion; she had chosen him in the maturity of her judgment; she had no fear but that he was of honest descent; and, in spite of old scandals, in spite of the shop, it was her firm intention to unite herself to him. For a short time the brothers were silent; but again they came forward triumphantly against Williams, full of the most fearful anxiety for their sister. They had been making inquiries—a rumour had reached them, they were themselves convinced of the truth of it—Williams was the son of a convict swindler! the son of that Edwards who was transported sixteen years ago for forgery. He had been adopted by the Osbornes, and did not bear even his own name! Their sister never should marry the son of a convict—they would oppose it in every way—she might turn Catholic, and enter a convent, but marry him she never should.

Thus the brothers wrote to her, and at the very same time poor Edwards wrote to his son a letter of humility and prayer. He was ill, he said: his daughter was wearing herself away over her work, which brought her no profit. If he, the son, would only allow them a hundred pounds a year, to be paid by a respectable banker, they would quit the town for ever, to live in some quiet, secluded place, where he should never hear of them more. Oh! for the love of mercy, would he but do this?

This letter was returned unopened and unanswered, and it was at this crisis that poor Edwards, as we have seen, disheartened and disappointed, left home with his camlet bag for an absence of two or three days. Williams was by no means in an easy state of mind, when a letter came to him from Miss Bassett, which, as we may believe, considerably agitated him. It was short, but still it said much. "Mere rank," she said, "was of no value in her mind, nor was great wealth; and, therefore, as he knew, she had made light of her brothers' objections against him on the score of his being of ordinary birth, and connected with trade: but an unsullied name and a fearlessly upright character were another thing; she now, therefore, put it to him solemnly, as he would answer before heaven—No; she would not put it thus," she said, "she would merely put it to his honour, to his regard for her, was he, or was he not, the son of that unhappy convict, Edwards, who was married to Miss Phillips, the sister of Mrs. Osborne?"

Terror now fell upon him strong as an armed man. His first thought was to get his father out of the way at any cost. He actually went to Mrs. Cope's, and asked to see him. He was out—his daughter was out; there was nothing to be done then, and, therefore, he sat down and wrote his answer to the lady, whom he was resolved not to lose. He talked of malice, and false friendship, and base attempts which were made to ruin him in her eyes, all which he said he defied. He deplored himself as the most unfortunate of men, because having been early left an orphan, he himself had not known his parents. He prized an unsullied name as much as she did, and would make one for himself. With her love, and for her

love, he could do anything; without it he should be
the veriest outcast in the world! *He was not the son
of that unfortunate man, Edwards!* and he earnestly
besought. her to close her ears against that malice
which was bent upon ruining him. "He felt," he said,
" that, once united, they should be happy; till then,
endless plans would be formed to separate them. Might
he beseech of her at once to set this malice at defiance
by allowing their marriage to take place immediately."

It was a bold letter. He trembled as he despatched
it. The next post brought him an answer. "Thank
you; you have taken a load from my heart. I knew
that you had not willingly deceived me, and I believe
you. But, Edward, shall I now confess my weakness
—had you, fearing to speak a falsehood, even for a
great reward, said, ' Yes, I am the son of that unhappy
convict, and in reality I bear his name,'—I could not
have abandoned you. Oh, my friend, you have gained
great power over me—you are very dear to me, and
I would have stood by your side to the last; and if the
world had upbraided you, it should have upbraided
me also. But, thank God, it need not be so. I will
be candid with you. My brothers are extremely
inveterate against you. Their consent to our marriage
will not be obtained, I fear. I wish to see you soon.
Come over for an hour to-morrow."

'There are no reproofs to a heart not naturally bad,
so severe as those of kindness. Williams sat silent
and self-accused. All his life long it seemed to him
that he had lived in the midst of kindness, which ho
had ill requited. He thought of Jessie Bannerman—
oh how often had Miss Bassett reminded him of Jessie
in her calm truthfulness! he thought of his good
aunt and uncle, how he had cheated and deceived

them. He was a moral coward; he had not the courage to do right—and he sat now humbled and chastised by his conscience. Oh that I had dared to speak the truth! Oh that I had but had the courage to speak the truth—that I had but had faith in the real greatness and goodness of her soul! I am a liar and a cheat, let me bear as fair a face to the world as I may, and a day will come when all my falsehood will come to light!

The next day he set off to the Forest for the interview which she desired, but not before he again made inquiries after the lodger at Mrs. Cope's, but the lodger was not returned, and, racked with the apprehension of something terrible hanging over him, he set out. He was prepared for some dreadful catastrophe, and felt more like a criminal going to judgment, than a lover on his way to arrange with a loving mistress for an early marriage. But what whips and stings has an evil conscience—how it torments with everlasting suggestions; suppose Miss Bassett should meet him with the full knowledge of all his baseness—suppose his father had actually been with her brothers, or herself—suppose he should be there with her, and she should confront them face to face! What should he do? Had he not now better go and throw himself at her feet, and confess all? Could she indeed love him after such a proof of his weakness? Or should he boldly adhere to his lie, and dare all consequences? He could not tell—he knew not what to do—he was like a weed on the tempested water, tossed here and there. A bitter curse is a mind ever wavering between right and wrong! and thus— miserable, vacillating, apprehensive, repentant, and yet ready to commit fresh sin to save himself, he went on.

As he rode slowly up through the plantations to the front of the cottage, a tall, but bending figure, was slowly passing down a side walk from the back premises. The rusty, but well-preserved black suit, the old hat, the blue camlet bag, he recognised them instantly. It was as if a dagger had pierced through his heart. He stopped his horse instantly—he had better at once fly than face her—his father had really been there—had revealed all, no doubt—he had not yet been seen from the house—there was time to fly —shame and terror overwhelmed him.

" Good morning, sir," said the cheerful voice of the gardener. " Shall I lead your horse up to the stable ? Missis is in the little flower-garden."

The gardener's voice reassured him, so did his words ; Miss Bassett was in the garden—she had not, then, seen his father. " What a coward apprehension has made of me !" thought he, and rode up to the house, bidding the gardener say nothing of his being come, and he would join Miss Bassett presently.

He was glad of this respite to recover himself ; the servants received him like a welcome guest at the house ; servants by instinct learn the tone of their employers' feelings—he knew that at present all was right.

" What did the old man want, with the blue bag, who was here just now ? " asked he.

" He has left a packet for the lady," the servant replied.

" The packet is for me—let me have it instantly," said he in a spasm of fear. " Fly, quick ! "

The servant, interpreting his impatience to be that of a lover, flew quickly, as he desired, to put into his hand one of those small packets of stationery which poor Edwards carried about. "To the inhabitant of this house," he read on the outside. Again there seemed something pitiful in his fear. There was nothing but innocent pens, sealing-wax, and wafers, inclosed in a wrapper, on which was printed, "All these for one shilling. The maker, who humbly solicits the benevolent to purchase, will call again to-morrow."

"The man is poor, very poor," said Williams, wrapping up the box again. "When he calls, give him this," said he, giving the servant a guinea—"he is very poor, though importunately troublesome; bid him not to come here again, however!"

Miss Bassett, so far from having any quarrel with her lover, or any suspicion of wrong against him, received him with the most marked, yet delicate kindness. Not one word did she say of the painful subject of their letters, but she spoke with tears of the harshness and unkindness of her brothers. They had quarrelled with her—she had no hope of reconciliation with them—she wished to leave the neighbourhood. Williams proposed their immediate marriage—she made no opposition—she felt as if she had no friend but himself. They arranged their plans rapidly. Williams, amazed at his own good fortune, was quite at his ease. The marriage, it was agreed, should take place, secretly, early in the next week—they would go at once to London, and from thence her brothers should know that their opposition was useless, and from London they would go to the Continent, where they would remain till the family displeasure had cooled.

Whilst thus arranging so agreeably his affairs with his affianced bride, his mind was busy about his

father, and he formed a plan, which, under the better
feeling inspired by the secret influence of this excellent woman, was not without kindness.   He gave a
sealed paper to the servant, which he ordered her
to give to the man, and then, after waiting to ascer-
tain that it was delivered into his hand, he took
leave of his bride, to meet her again only for the
marriage.

From the Forest Lodge he went to the Three
Queens, in Burton, where, as he expected, the poor
man with the camlet bag was not long in making his
appearance also.   They had a long interview, which
ended apparently most amicably.   They both left
Burton that night—Edwards by one coach, and his
son by another.

CHAPTER IV.

THEY ARE OFF.—THEY ARE MARRIED.

IT was two days after this before he reached home.
He came by the Birmingham coach, but he was so
entirely his own master, that nobody ever thought
of asking wherefore he had been there.   Reynolds,
however, who had been looking for him every hour
since the discovery he had made regarding his sister,
met him at the shop-door with that sort of impatient
good-news countenance, which seems to say, "Here I
am! ask me what I have got to tell!" But Williams
did not ask, and at last Reynolds, who could contain
no longer, invited him to a private conference, and
then began in a low voice of the most heartfelt joy—
"I say, my good fellow, do you know that your sister
is in this town? The most beautiful little angel that
ever was seen, and as good as she is beautiful! And

9

do you know," added he in a more measured tone, "that—your father is here too?"

Williams turned pale as death, and Reynolds attributing this to shame regarding his father's disgrace, wished he only knew how to show his good and kind intentions. "I am sure, my dear fellow," he began, "if I were in your place, I would not let it trouble me a bit; the world need not know anything about it; and to make you quite at ease with me on the subject, I will confess something to you. I too have had sorrow in my family, and deeper sorrow than yours, for here is your father come back, with time, and opportunity, and willingness to retrieve his character in life. My poor father, alas, had not time hardly to repent. You and I are old friends; there need be no secrets between us, though nobody else need know about your poor father—nobody, indeed, ever dreams that this is your father—nobody but Miss Kendricks and myself."

"What, in the fiend's name, does all this mean?" demanded Williams, again assaulted on this fearful subject from a quarter where he least expected it.

"What does it mean?" repeated Reynolds, quite taken aback. "Why, that your father is come back, and that your sister is here, and that my aunt Kendricks can see in her a strong likeness to your mother."

Reynolds had never in his life before mentioned to Williams suspicions of his parentage, and he now said, "I've known it long, Williams, that Edwards was your father, and it's no use trying to impose upon me; nor really, if you knew me, would you think it needful to try; so let us deal openly with one another—here are your father and sister."

"They are impostors," interrupted Williams, in a low, but firm voice. "Arch impostors; and don't you go and let your good-nature believe every artful lie that is told you. They are impostors, I tell you; I have seen him, and I am mistaken if he be not off pretty handily."

"And do you actually pretend not to believe it?" cried Reynolds, growing quite warm. "I appeal to your conscience, Williams, whether, in the face of heaven, you dare to disown them. They are not impostors, and that you know! How dare you, with your plenty,—or even if you had to slave for your daily bread it would be the same thing,—how dare you cast your father into poverty, perhaps into crime, and what is ten thousand times worse, cast that lovely creature, your own sister, who is pure as the very stars of heaven, friendless upon the world? I will stand between you and your pride, Williams, if pride it be, or your false shame, or want of moral courage, or whatever it is, and force you to do them right! They are your own flesh and blood, and as you hope for the blessing of God on your own life and undertakings, be just to them."

Williams heard all in gloomy silence, and then inquired where he had seen "these people."

Reynolds related what had occurred between Marianne and himself, and showed how the peculiar circumstances of his own early life had rendered him, as it were, innocently a party in the misunderstanding; he told how pleased his aunt Kendricks had been with her, and how they had kept her at their house for one, if not two, nights.

A peculiar smile passed over Williams's countenance, which Reynolds could not understand. "What a fool the girl must be, if this be not a double-dyed piece of artifice," said he. "And how famously you have been imposed upon!"

With these words he left him, and Reynolds, burning with indignation at what he felt to be his cold-blooded pride, felt, nevertheless, an uncomfortable query in his own heart—"And can I, after all, have been duped?"

"No! no! no!" said every sense of honesty and sincerity in his own breast. "As soon would I disbelieve the sun in heaven as that girl." He was sure he was right, and, within half an hour, set off to Mrs. Cope's, to see both father and daughter. He was bent upon obtaining from them such evidences as Williams should not gainsay. He knew enough of Williams to believe him capable of prevarication and falsehood, but he had great faith also in the good that was in him, and on that he resolved to work—in the meantime he must see these two—he wanted to see father and daughter together, to question and cross-question, to know how they were in health, to cheer up their spirits, in short, he was for the first time in his life in love—he wanted to see his mistress.

Williams on his part did not trouble himself about them. He had plenty of business of other kinds on his hands. He was busy about his marriage. He wrote to his banker, to his lawyer, and to his tailor; there was a world of business to be done in the next few days.

Great was Reynolds's astonishment, and almost horror, when, on passing the little parlour window at Mrs. Cope's, he saw, instead of the miniatures, and profiles, and pretty bags and rugs, which were usually arranged there—two caps on wooden stands, and two pieces of printed cotton, and one of shot-silk, which were in progress of gown-making. Mrs. Cope was in possession of her little parlour again; her lodgers were gone!

"What; was he in your debt for sealing-wax and such things?" asked Mrs. Cope, in reply to Reynolds's sudden exclamation at hearing that they left the day before.

"Where are they gone?" he inquired.

Mrs. Cope could not tell; it seemed all a sudden thing; the old gentleman had come home after being away for three days. He seemed very poorly and out of spirits when he went, but when he came back he was quite another person; he sent out for half a pound of cheese, a beefsteak, and a pot of porter, and had a good supper. He seemed to have plenty of money; he was up all night packing up his things. The daughter was not half as cheerful; she sat painting at those things for Mrs. Bishop, and sweet pretty things they were. Mrs. Cope's girl took them home. Mrs. Bishop, she said, wanted something else painted, and she wished her to go there, and then she would pay her for them all together. The father, however, would not let her go, nor somewhere else, where she wanted to go, and she cried even—but the old gentleman was angry, and would not let her. He said there was not time. He said that he had met with a friend, and that they must meet him that day —so they went by coach to Lichfield, he outside, and she in. She seemed quite down-hearted at going, and said that Mrs. Cope must take, for her own trouble, the guinea and a half which Mrs. Bishop owed, and she had left a bag worked with beads, and a very pretty bunch of wax roses for Miss Kendricks, with her

love, and she should never forget their kindness.
Mrs. Cope said that she took shame to herself for not
having been down with them, but one of her young
women was ill, and she was so full of work—but she
meant, if she could get a bit of time, to take them
that night.

Reynolds said that he would save her the trouble,
that he was going to his aunt's, and would carry them
with him.

Mrs. Cope's tidings quite upset him—he thought of
Williams's words—" They are impostors. I have
seen him, and I am mistaken if they are not speedily
off." Off they certainly were, and he had no doubt
but that Williams had a hand in it; but that they
were impostors he could not believe. His aunts
were of his opinion, and without knowing their
nephew's private reasons for anxiety, seconded all
that he said in behalf of their truth. It was impossible that they could be impostors, the young lady
was too much like her own mother for that. Oh no ;
Williams knew very well where they were ; he had
sent them out of the way, and, no doubt, would
provide for them ; there seemed to them nothing so
strange in his wishing them not to appear just now.
Did not people say that he was paying his addresses
to Lawyer Bassett's sister? They could understand
exactly how it was, only they must confess that he
need not have told lies to an old friend, like their
nephew, that he might have known would never
make mischief or betray him in any way. But it was
like Williams, they said, and they had no right to be
surprised at it.

Reynolds became again easy in his mind, and
returned home to prepare for the morrow, which was

May-fair day, when they would all be busy with
country customers.   He did not see Williams again
that night, but he resolved on the very first opportunity to place the utmost confidence in him as regarded
himself; to confess his love for his sister, which he
could not doubt being agreeable to him, and obtaining
from him a knowledge of their residence, to lose no
time in making her an offer of his heart and hand.
He would by this means prove to Williams how little
he thought of the painful past as regarded his father
—nay, on his marriage, he would enter into a bond
on behalf of his wife, to make some provision for the
old man.   He would in every way do that which was
generous and honourable, and this he would tell Williams.   Nothing puts one in such good humour with
one's-self and all the world as the intention of doing
something remarkably generous, especially when one
can serve one's-self at the same time.   It was this
feeling which made Reynolds alert and cheerful all
the day.   The country people said, "What a nice
gentleman he was!"   He listened to all kinds of
weariful histories about diseases in cattle and children,
and old folks; he prescribed for dry-rot in houses,
and the fly in turnips; he did not sell even a pennyworth of turmeric without a pleasant word.   Every
customer was charmed with him; he "quite cut
out" their old favourite, Mr. Isaacs, who happened to
be rather out of humour that day, it must be confessed.   At the end of the day, Mr. Reynolds informed
his partner that there never had been such a day
since he had known the shop; it had been quite
crowded all day : and on adding up the day's receipts,
besides booking, it was half as much again as that
day last year.

Mr. Isaacs said it need, for that Williams had suddenly called for two hundred pounds out of the business, which he said had worried him no little. Williams was gone off with a good deal of luggage, and had said that he should not be back at present, but that he would write. Here was news of astonishment for Reynolds! He was gone, no doubt, after his father and sister; the two hundred pounds was for their use; he was gone to settle them comfortably somewhere; he rose at once fifty per cent. in his young partner's estimation; he was welcome to draw two hundred pounds from the business; Reynolds would almost have given it to him. These were his thoughts, and he replied cheerfully to his senior, "Well, I don't see that we need trouble ourselves about that; he takes no part in the business now, and we are just as well without him as with him."

" But," said Mr. Isaacs angrily, " it 's an unpleasant thing to have money drawn out at a minute's warning —to be sure the firm has money in the bank—but with his twenty thousand pounds—and he a bachelor —he should not do it !"

" Here is news !" exclaimed Reynolds within a very few days, looking up from the London paper which he was reading. "Now listen, Mr. Isaacs, and I shall amaze you,— and he read—' On Saturday, the 7th inst., at St. George's, Hanover Square, Edward Lewis Williams, Esquire, of Utceter, to Emmeline, sole daughter of the late George Vernon Bassett, Esquire, of Henshall Hall, Staffordshire.' "

" And he really is married, is he ?" exclaimed the old man. "At St. George's, Hanover Square ! Bless me !"

" Well, here's a bit of news !" exclaimed all the

Mrs. Proctors and Mrs. Morleys of Utceter and of Burton-on-Trent. " Here's a bit of news that will take a deal of talking over. Married are they after a six weeks' courtship, and she gone off to London, pious as she was reckoned, all on the sly, with only her maid ; why, it is not much better than being married at Gretna Green ;" and everybody's tongue was set in motion.

" And she really *has* married him after all !" exclaimed the two brothers Bassett. "*After all,* has married the son of a convict ! Well, we hope they'll go abroad, and live abroad too, and never come back again !"

" And yet," said they a week after the first anger, " we must net say anything about his father—for the credit of the family we must not ! And, seeing she was determined to marry him, it was almost a pity that we said so much—but after all it was only among ourselves, so there is no great harm done—but we wish to heaven that they may live abroad altogether !"

The new Mrs. Williams wrote from London to her brother at Burton, and informed him that it was the joint wish of herself and her husband that the Lodge should be now let for a term of years; that the furniture should be sold by auction, and her books, pictures, musical instruments, &c., should be deposited in the hands of certain persons whom she named. It was their intention, she said, to be absent for some years, and she felt sure that her dear brother, in accordance with his usual kindness to her, would transact this business for them, and it was the wish of her husband that he (the lawyer) should remunerate himself for all his trouble out of the rent, which might lie in his hands till called for.

It was evidently the intention of Mr. and Mrs. Williams to keep up a good understanding with her family; the family were satisfied that it should be so, but, as a means of keeping them abroad, they soon found a good tenant, for a term of years, for the very pretty Forest Lodge.

CHAPTER V.

ANOTHER OLD ACQUAINTANCE.

We hope our readers are disposed to like Mrs. Williams; she was a good woman; she had some of those sterling qualities which he had not, but which always in others had a great influence on him; it is strange to say it, but it is, nevertheless, true, her first charm to his feelings was that singular transparency and evident truthfulness of mind and character which he had always felt so strongly in Jessie Bannerman. They both had the power of awakening the better part of his nature, of producing in him, as it were, an acquiescence to good. He had deceived his wife, it is true; he had fallen into the gulf of falsehood, that fatal gulf which, it seemed to him, ever lay before him. And oh, what a bitter weight of self-condemnation lay upon his soul for it; how did it come between him and his happiness, between her love and his peace of mind. "*Would that I had wist!*" is the most painful expression of a saddened spirit—for it implies that we have been the fashioners of our own anguish.

We must now see them in London. All the world was then talking of Mademoiselle Angela. She was a young actress; the most beautiful of women, according to report, and the most accomplished of actresses. She had been abroad, in Petersburgh and Paris, and had created an extraordinary sensation there. Her fame had come before her: people who had seen her abroad raved about her in London, and now she was come, in the month of May, in the full blaze of the London season, and had at once taken the heart of the whole town. Her portraits were in the windows; she set the fashion in caps and gowns; her voice, her attitudes, her smiles were the theme of every one's admiration; but, more than all, was talked of her beautiful character. Her life, it was said, had been as strange as a fairy tale; she had gone through poverty, hardship, and temptation of every kind, but all had been unable to tarnish the pure gold of her nature. She was, fame said, the most gifted and best of human beings; people told endless anecdotes about her; her life was so pure, yet brilliant, and people were so enthusiastic about her, that one might have thought her sent down from heaven to make goodness fashionable.

Mrs. Williams, who had from principle a terror of the stage, refused, spite of the entreaties of their London acquaintance, to attend the theatre. Chance had led them among a circle of people who were most theatrically inclined, and who were going to one theatre or another every night. Williams, who had a strong desire to join them, declined, for some time, from regard to his wife. She became aware, however, at length, of the self-denial he had practised for her sake, and insisted upon it that he should go to see this wonderful phœnix, of which the world talked so much. He was to accompany a party, which was to occupy one of the stage-boxes. The gentlemen took with them bouquets and wreaths of flowers, to fling as offerings at the feet of the queen of the night : rings, it was said, and ornaments of great value, had frequently been conveyed to her feet in this way, and Mrs. Williams gave to her husband a small wreath of myrtle and jasmine, which, she said, if he found her to be as beautiful as she was said to be good, he was to fling to her also.

A strange, bewildering, dream-like feeling came over Williams as he stood behind the row of ladies of their party, waiting for the drawing up of the curtain. The orchestra played Mozart's overture to Don Juan. His mind went back to those strange, far-off days when he stood in the little theatre at Utceter, waiting for the drawing up of the curtain, to see her whom he then reckoned the angel of his life. Fancy is a very powerful and a very deceptive thing ; the great house seemed to dwarf itself down to the dimensions of the little one—the gay audience were the dowdy gentry of a country-town. The huge curtain drew up, and there, like the glorified image of the heroine of former days, stood the splendidly attired, and serenely beautiful Mademoiselle Angela. The whole house rose, and the gentlemen shouted for very enthusiasm ; the ladies waved their handkerchiefs, and the newspapers of the next morning said that nothing could exceed the rapture with which the young actress was received.

"I protest! ' exclaimed one of the gentlemen in their box, "that Williams has been standing like a mummy all this time."

Poor Williams ! and there was good reason why he had done so. A dizziness had come over him ; he fancied that he must have fainted, but nobody then observed it. They said now that he looked pale; he said that the theatre was so hot.

Everybody was engrossed by the piece, and he too looked on. It *was* Jessie Bannerman; he saw it plainly; the same being, who, sitting with him in the patten-maker's parlour, had told him her sad history; the same who had gone with him on that Christmas-day to Alton Towers; who had made that strange compact with him of trial and fidelity for five years; the same who had been true to him for five years, and then offered him, herself, her love and her gratitude, and had been rejected by him; and who, with her love and gratitude, had he but been worthy of them, would have conferred upon him wealth, splendour, honour, the world's renown, only to have been allied to her.

The piece was Othello. And now she came to the second scene of the fourth act, where Desdemona, on her knees before Othello, asserts her innocence.

She seemed to surpass even herself; the public enthusiasm rose to the highest pitch; flowers were rained down from every box near the stage, and came flying from pit and gallery.

"Now, Williams, fling down your garland to her," resounded distinctly on the stage from the box above. She cast her eye in the direction of the voice instantly; their eyes met, it was but for a moment, but to Williams it seemed as if he had shrunk into nothingness before the clear, keen gaze of those beautiful eyes. He groaned inwardly; he felt how little, how mean he was; how wretched, how despicable had been all his aims in life. She rose higher and higher; there was a majesty in her action, a thrilling tone in her voice that crushed him. He felt at once humbled

before her ; he felt again, as he had felt before, that
high moral tone in her, which, combined with great
intellectual power, is the very essence of the divine
nature.

"How omnipotent is goodness! how godlike."
he exclaimed inwardly. "How could I ever have
been worthy of her!"

He stood, and gazed upon her, and wept like a
child. People seemed to take no notice of him, they
were so occupied by her and by themselves.

The theatre-going world said that she had never
acted so well as on that night.

This discovery of Jessie Bannerman in the renowned
Mademoiselle Angela was not a circumstance calculated to add to Williams's matrimonial happiness. He
drew invidious comparisons between the favourite
actress and his wife, between himself now and that
which he might have been had he married her. He
was enraged with himself; called himself fool and
blockhead, and made himself very unhappy.

At the end of the month, as had been at first proposed, Mrs. Williams insisted on their going to Paris;
she was tired of hearing of Mademoiselle Angela; she
did not like her husband going so continually to the
theatre, where she never accompanied him ; according
to her notions of things, it was not right.

To Paris, therefore, they went.

"Edward, my love," said his wife to him one day,
not long after their arrival there, "will you be my
father confessor?"

"Can you, who are so good, have anything to confess?" he exclaimed.

"Listen," she said, "and you shall hear. I was
jealous of Mademoiselle Angela." He started. "Nay,

upon my word," she said, " you will make me think that I had cause. . Mrs. Moorwood told me of your agitation when you saw her first. You know not, Edward," she said, "the anguish I have felt; I fancied that you were cold to me ; I fancied that your heart seemed turned from me—there is something so entire, so true in a woman's love, Edward, and I was jealous of that fair Angela, who seemed to have deprived me of yours in return. Now I have been candid with you. I have told you my weakness ; let there never be suspicion between us, and, as a proof that your love is not diminished, tell me, was Mademoiselle Angela known to you before ?"

. Without replying, he looked into his wife's face. His first impulse was to deny altogether the truth of her suspicion—was to deny any knowledge of the actress.

" Edward," continued she, solemnly, " answer me truly—love and falsehood cannot exist in the same bosom. The happiness of our whole life may depend on this moment—do not deceive me ! You have loved Mademoiselle Angela !"

Again he felt that singular resemblance between his wife and Angela—that spirit of truth which had made him submissive before the spirit of a girl in former years. He felt that, sustained by this spirit, he dared to speak the truth, even to his own condemnation.

" Yes," he said, " you are right ; I have loved her —and, perhaps, love her still ; but oh ! Emmeline, since we have thus spoken, you need not fear her. Truth is, indeed, a broad shield against sin. You need not fear her. I love her less dangerously, and you more truly. But you shall hear all." He then related that which the reader already knows; perhaps not in its fullest details—perhaps disguising a little of his own weakness—but still with that sufficient adherence to truth as left him guilty. Emmeline sat with her calm eyes fixed upon him—she did not speak one word to interrupt him.

"Thank you, my beloved," said she, when he had finished, and when, overcome by emotion, he sank his face upon his hands, and wept. "Thank you, from this day forth a new covenant is made between us. We shall neither of us err greatly while we have courage to face the truth. You have given me the greatest proof of your love by placing confidence in me. May God Almighty enable me to make you happy!" She sank her head on the shoulder of her husband, and wept with him.

A new era in the life of our married pair might be dated from this time. Mademoiselle Angela was never mentioned between them, but she was the bond of their better understanding. One thing only embittered Williams's life; that was his falsehood regarding his father. Often and often he was on the point of confessing the whole terrible truth, and his own culpable weakness, but then he dared not; she seemed so happy, she had such faith in him, the knowledge of this must blast all. It lay like a festering sore on his soul, and led him only into new difficulties and deceptions. He dreaded the arrival of letters; his wife showed him all hers, and seemed to expect the same from him. She was one of those clear-headed, straightforward women who have a capacity for business; she took the management of all their present affairs into her hands, and her husband, who had a decided distaste for business of every kind, was quite willing that she should do so. But now and then came letters which she must not see. Reynolds wrote to him, begging most urgently for the address of that person who called himself Jervis; why he wanted it, he did not say, but stated merely that it was on a matter of vital importance to himself. This letter put Williams in a state of the greatest uneasiness; for what purpose could Reynolds want the address? Were the Bassetts reviving the old subject? Was Reynolds himself going to meddle in it? He wrote back a short reply. He knew nothing of the person calling himself Jervis, farther than that, to prevent the circulation of reports unpleasant to himself, he had caused him to remove to Birmingham. Reynolds must remember that he, Williams, had always considered him an impostor.

Next came a letter from Williams's father. He had obtained the address from the banker in London, who was empowered to pay his allowance. He wrote from Bath, whither he had removed from Birmingham, in consequence of the illness of his daughter. He had been obliged to consult physicians for her; her illness was expensive to him. He must trouble his son for a further advance of money to meet this exigency.

This letter, even more than the former, discomposed him, and, to silence this most fearful of correspondents, he sent him an order on his banker, not, however, without forbidding any further application to himself; and to his banker he also wrote, forbidding his address in future being furnished to this his annuitant.

After this, Williams changed his lodgings, and did not in future allow his letters to come to his residence. Early in the next year he removed from Paris to Vienna.

On the second day of their being in this city, and whilst yet at the inn, one of those singular coincidences occurred which are by no means as unfrequent as some persons imagine. They dined, as is customary, in a public room, where many persons were dining at separate tables. A party of gentlemen sat at a table beside them; they were English, and were ta king loudly. One of them was a Mr. Burndale, of London, a banker, and the conversation was about forgeries, when Mr. Burndale was appealed to

" By the bye, Burndale," said one of the gentlemen, " is it true that that fellow, Edwards, whom you transported some sixteen or eighteen years ago, for a forgery on your bank, is come back, and has opened some sort of eating-house or tavern at the West End ?"

Long before thus much had been said, Williams felt as if the soup which he was eating would choke him. His wife, too, had heard what was said, and was almost as much agitated as himself; for she knew that this was the man with whom her brothers had connected her husband.

" Are you not well, love," said she, tenderly; " shall we leave the room ?"

He was not unwell, he said hastily, and called for wine, and the gentlemen went on : " Yes, it was quite true; he was come back; somebody had advanced him money, and he had actually opened a tavern or gaming-house, or something of the kind; it was astonishing," they said, " how some people got on through life."

Williams drank wine and made the most violent
efforts to look composed, and to a great degree he
succeeded. His wife remembered what had passed
between them on the subject before their marriage,
and his agitation appeared natural ; she began a most
cheerful conversation with him, and used every effort
in her power to drive away all unpleasant thoughts.

The next day they left the inn. Mrs. Williams
was expecting to become a mother in a few months ;
they, therefore, took a suite of rooms for the summer,
intending before winter to remove to Florence, where
they proposed taking up their abode.

One thought for ever haunted Williams, and that
was his father, and the discovery which, sooner or
later, his wife would make. He loved her extremely ;
Mademoiselle Angela was no longer her rival ; he
would have given thousands, that he only had never
deceived her ; but every day made it more difficult
now to confess the truth. His letters never came to
the house ; he dreaded going into public lest he should
be recognised in some way ; he was become the slave
of perpetual apprehension. He bought a horse and
rode violently ; it was the only thing that seemed to
remove him from himself; yet he never returned
home without fearing that the frightful secret was
out. .All this preyed upon his health ; he looked ill
and haggard ; his wife grew anxious about him ; he
assumed spirits which he did not feel, and was all the
time miserable. To add to his anxiety, Reynolds
still pursued him with letters, and at length came in
person. He came with the most resolute purpose of
dragging from Williams the secret of his father's
residence. He came with tidings for which Williams

was not prepared—the happiness of his life depended upon his marriage with Williams's sister—he would not speak of her in any other character than as his sister; he defied him, before Heaven, to deny that she was so, or that *her* father was other than *his*. He was so firm, so much in earnest, that Williams quailed before him. Life and death, he said, was in his errand, and he would not be trifled with. He only wanted to be enabled to find them, and then Williams might cast them off for ever—might disown them—might lie before God and man; they should from that day want neither friend nor support, for he himself would maintain them. Williams told him honestly that which he knew; he had established them as he hoped permanently in Birmingham, and had secured to them a hundred a year by quarterly payments. They had left Birmingham, however, and gone to Bath, and after that he had incidentally learned they were in London, where the father had opened some kind of tavern at the West End—a mad, foolish scheme, said Williams, and that was honestly all he knew. Reynolds, on his part, knew as much, which he related: he had traced them from town to town, and at length to London, where, as was stated, the father had been unwise enough to enter into some sort of scheme, but not in a tavern or gaming-house, in what was designed for a small respectable coffee-house and news-room. He had had a stroke, however, which incapacitated him from business. The whole place was broken up—all was complete ruin—and after that, he and his daughter seemed lost amid the vastness of sorrow and disappointed hopes in London. Reynolds was a man, physically and morally, with nerves as of iron; he was not to be daunted by difficulties, or impeded by obstacles of one kind or another, and now he stood before Williams like the personification of determined will, and demanded from him where was his sister?

"Would to Heaven I could tell you!" said Williams, with sincerity.

Reynolds did not believe him. Williams tried every means in his power to convince him; offered him an unlimited order on his banker for their use; but Reynolds rejected it. "It is a mockery," said he, indignantly, "to offer money now, when you have compelled them into unknown misery and perhaps ruin!"

A violent quarrel ensued, and Reynolds returned to England, cursing what he considered the heartless, selfish, unnatural pride and unkindness of his partner, and resolved to spend his life, if needful, in rescuing the girl he loved so tenderly from the misery which seemed to encompass her.

It was impossible to keep from Mrs. Williams's knowledge the fact that something unpleasant had caused this unexpected journey of her husband's partner to such a distance, and no doubt Williams would have found the concealment of the truth much more difficult than he did, had not fortune favoured him; his child was born, and the mother forgot every unpleasant thing in the joy of her first-born.

Months went on. A house was taken for them at Florence; the day fixed for their journey was come. At the moment of departure a letter from England was put into Williams's hand; it was in a woman's hand-writing, and had been sent merely directed to his name through the English ambassador. It was from his sister, and was a most touching appeal to his humanity, if not to his affection. Her father, she said, had lost the use of one side; had lost his memory completely, and in part his speech—he was a pitiable and infirm object. She was making the most gigantic efforts in her power for their support; but she had no friends. She knew not the banking-house whence her father drew their quarterly payments, and her father's efforts to recall it were hopeless. Her own health was giving way, and she besought him, without loss of time, in the name of that Great Father before whom they must all one day answer for their deeds, to inform her of the name of his banker, and thus rescue them from the horrible misery which already stared them in the face. His heart was wrung as he hastily perused it. His wife came in at that moment; the carriage was at the door; the servants and the courier came bustling about; his wife said all was ready, and she was impatient to be off; he crumpled the letter hastily in his hand, gave his arm to his wife, and placed her in the carriage; the nurse and the child followed quickly, all was bustle and confusion; he took his seat; there were yet cloaks, and shawls, and travelling baskets, and little bags, and endless things to be looked after, for Mrs. Williams was one of those provident persons who cared for every want beforehand. Scarcely were they off, when Williams recalled the letter; it was not in his hand—it had not been in his hand for some time—where had he put it? He was alarmed; he quietly felt his own pockets, looked behind his wife, looked behind the nurse, but it was not to be seen.

He dared not ask about it, but sat troubled and uneasy in the corner of his carriage, trying to recal to his recollection what had occurred but a few moments before. That he had it crumpled up in his hand as he assisted his wife into the carriage he could recollect; but his mind was so agitated and bewildered at the moment that he knew not what he did; he could remember nothing more about it till he had missed it; he feared that he had dropped it in getting into the carriage, and in that case it would be found and might be made public—might be sent after him --nay, he could not tell what might be the consequence; but that which seemed even worse than this, was the chance of his never finding it, for thus he had not the slightest idea of what the address was, to which his reply should be sent. It was a most agonising thought. He hoped, however, that it might still be in the carriage among its various contents. At the first place they stopped he had everything taken out—but no letter was there!

They came to their journey's end; took possession of their new house—a beautiful prince-like villa on the banks of the Arno; his wife was happy; the child was lovely, and throve like a flower in May; she was the fondest of mothers. Could she but have seen her husband happy, she would have been the happiest of wives. As at Vienna so here, he spent most of his time on horseback; he was as little as possible at home. Had his wife's mind been less occupied by the child than it was, she never would have rested without penetrating the secret of his sadness. But when she saw him at home, she saw him with assumed spirits, and she had no idea of his hours of secret, untold agony of mind; she saw that there was something wrong, and with all the power of her love she tried to set it right; she carefully kept from him every painful subject, met him ever with smiles, and tried all in her power to make him happy.

He in the meantime had written to Vienna about the lost letter; instituted all kind of search, and offered reward, but to no purpose. The letter did not appear, and the thought of the paralytic, speech-less man, and the young girl thrown friendless on the heartless world of London, haunted him day and night. Oh, how bitterly was he punished. He was willing now to help them—nay, to make any sacri-fice for them, and he had lost the power of doing so. He thought of old Mrs. Bellamy's words, " children, children, never let pass an opportunity of doing a kindness to those you ought to love, or the time may come when the thought of not having done so will pursue you as with a whip of scorpions ! "

CHAPTER VI.

MADEMOISELLE ANGELA.

The newspapers announced one morning that, in consequence of the severe illness of the grandmother of Mademoiselle Angela, that favourite actress would not perform that evening as usual. The public, who lost a night's pleasure in consequence of the old lady's illness, sincerely wished her better—but the wish availed nothing; the old lady died.

" Mademoiselle Angela desires to have some one

sent to her to alter her mourning, to-day," said Mr. Jones, of one of the great mourning warehouses in London, to his head man ; " see that some one is sent to her immediately." The head man communicated the order to the principal work-woman, adding, " that she had better send one of the cleverest hands." The principal work-woman glanced into the large room, where there sat thirty young women at their gloomy trade, and without waiting to make any selection, called out that " Miss Jervis must take her working materials and go instantly to Mademoiselle Angela and make such alterations in her mourning as she required." It was an every-day occurrence, and the young lady to whom the commission was given having prepared all that was needful to take with her, which were contained in a little black box, found a cab waiting for her at the shop-door, and drove off to the handsome house of the renowned actress.

A man-servant conducted her up-stairs, and there a grave, middle-aged waiting-woman received her, who led her into Mademoiselle Angela's own bed-room. The chamber was the handsomest that the young work-woman had ever seen, and she was rather excited, for she knew how renowned was the lady to whom it belonged ; her very heart beat at the thought of seeing her. The rich mourning lay on the bed, and while she took off her bonnet and cloak, Mademoiselle Angela entered.

" How beautiful she is, and how good she looks," thought poor Marianne.

The great lady smiled kindly at the young, modest dressmaker—she too was struck by her appearance ; a sentiment of great kindness filled her heart—

she made up her mind instantly as to what she
would do.

The young girl sat down to the work which was
pointed out to her, and Mademoiselle Angela, order-
ing a book to be brought to her, and dismissing the
woman, with the desire that no one should interrupt
her that morning, seated herself on the sofa, and
began to read.   The room was so still that the quick
movement of Marianne's needle and the turning of
the pages of the book were audible.   At length
Mademoiselle Angela, closing the book, said, "Yours
is a melancholy occupation ; all day long, the whole
year through, working for sorrow, or what is worse,
the mockery of sorrow."

The young girl sighed.

"It must be," continued the actress, "a weary
trade to you."

"I am," said Marianne, "so thankful to be
employed, that to me it is not so."

"Have you then known distress?" asked the other,
but in so kind a tone that Marianne continued—

"I have a father dependent upon me—we have
been very unfortunate," she said, hardly keeping back
the tears ; "very unfortunate in many ways. I have
feared starvation almost for us both, I have feared—
Oh, I cannot tell what I have feared—London is an
awful place for any one who is friendless—for a young
girl especially."

The actress laid down her book, and taking a chair
sat down by the table where the girl was working.

"I am a stranger to you," she said, very kindly;
" you know nothing of me ; can feel no reason why
you should make a confidant of me—yet I wish you
would do so."

The girl sighed again, and wiped away the tears which this kindness had called forth. " I have heard a great deal of you, Mademoiselle Angela," she said ; " everybody talks of you, and I have heard that you are very good, but I have nothing to tell you that can interest you much, there are alas, so many unfortunate people in London."

" The unfortunate are always interesting to me," said the actress, with that air of simple, emphatic truth which was her distinguishing characteristic.

Marianne felt its influence, and replied, " There are circumstances connected with my family which are of a painful and altogether private nature—my father, who is old in experience and sorrow, rather than in years, and who is now helpless as a child in mind and body, has been wholly dependent upon me for the last twelve months. He was extremely fond of me ; he expected that I should make my fortune by marriage ; what little money we have had he has risked to make more for my sake—and all has been lost ! We have now been in London a year and a half, and in that time I have tried endless means of obtaining our livelihood. I have been well educated, and as I know myself as well qualified for teaching as nine out of ten who do teach, I offered myself as daily governess, as teacher in a school, as instructor in various ways, but there always were for such situations twenty or more applicants besides myself, all of whom came supported by friends or interest of some kind or other. I had none. I tried to take pupils, but none came. I made fancy-work of all kinds, and taught it, but by this I lost money. I painted miniatures—children, dogs, cats, parrots, any-thing—and if dogs, cats, and parrots had alone been my subjects and sitters, I might have done; but a young lady, at least a poor one, cannot in London attempt this mode of gaining her living without being subjected to the most annoying insults. People," said she, blushing deeply, "thought me pretty, and in every way, in every situation, this was against me. Oh," said the poor girl, with tears in her eyes, "how often have I thought it would have been a blessing if I had the small-pox!"

"And have you no friends at all?" asked Mademoiselle Angela.

"Friends!" repeated she, blushing deeply and sighing; "friends! yes, perhaps so. We ought to receive an annuity, which would make us independent, but he who should pay it is abroad. Oh, it is a sad thing," said she, bursting into tears.

The actress was deeply interested, "And why does he not pay it?" she asked.

"I have written to him," replied she, "since my father's memory has failed him, and have told him all our distress; but he takes no notice."

"But have you not other friends?" she asked, "no connections, nobody that knows your family?"

Again the girl blushed: "Yes," she said, "there are two ladies, very good and kind, who showed me great kindness, who knew my mother—but circumstances forbid my applying to them—yet I do believe that if they only knew what I have suffered they would befriend me."

"Do they live in London?" asked the actress.

"No," she returned, "they live in the country, in Staffordshire."

"Could no one interfere for you—write to them for you?"

Marianne looked up from her work for a moment, and fixed her eyes on the lovely face of the actress and said, " perhaps they might, but— "

" I am curious about you," interrupted Mademoiselle Angela ; " I have been in Staffordshire— perhaps I know your friends—where do they live— tell me ?" she said in a manner so unlike her usual calmness, that Marianne again looked in her face. " I once knew some parts of Staffordshire ; tell me who are your friends, and where they live."

" They live at a small town called Uteeter," said Marianne ; " their name is Kendrick."

The actress rose instantly from her seat, and walked across the room — she seemed agitated — put her handkerchief to her face, and then sat down again.

" I told you," said she, hurriedly, " that I knew something of Staffordshire. " Uteeter I know, but not your friends. No," said she, in her usual calm and simple manner, " your friends, the Kendricks, I never knew."

Marianne ventured a remark which made her heart tremble. " There was a Mr. Osborne there," she said, " and a young Mr. Williams, his nephew— but I daresay you never knew them."

" Ah !" said the actress, with an emotion which made her cheeks as pale as marble ; " what of them —what of young Mr. Williams? Has he been a false lover of yours ? "

" Oh, no, no ?" said Marianne, looking at her in amazement; " but oh, Mademoiselle Angela, if you know anything of him—for he is a rich man now— for the love of God, do tell him that the old man— he knows who—is almost in want—would be in want

but for me—and I, what can I do? with all my
utmost exertion I can earn but fifteen shillings a
week. Oh, Mademoiselle Angela," said she, dropping
on her knees before her, "if you know him, do this
for the sake of Christian love ; oh, do it ! for if you
ask, who can resist you ?"

"Rise!" said the actress, deeply affected ; "rise,
my good girl. With the man you name I can do
nothing—but remember that I am your friend !"

With these words she went out, leaving poor
Marianne to her tears and her astonishment.

Two days after this a letter came to Miss Kendrick,
which excited the greatest astonishment and delight,
and well might it do so. It was from that celebrated
Mademoiselle Angela, whose fame had spread all over
England, and it told, as the incomparable Angela only
could tell it, the story of her acquaintance with
Marianne Jervis. Miss Kendrick, the letter said,
would know how they could best befriend her ; for
the present, however, this young girl was her inmate,
and her father, who was feeble and infirm in the last
degree, was about to be removed to one of those
blessed institutions — the Sanatorium — where for
invalids of the middle-class every comfort of home is
combined with the most skilful medical treatment.

What did Miss Kendrick do when she read this
letter ? First of all she had a good fit of crying, and
then she put on her bonnet and shawl and trotted off
to her nephew, to whom she knew its contents would
be like a message from Heaven.

The next day, though it was a market-day, Reynolds set off for London. "I shall be at home again

with all my faculties to attend to business for the future," said he. " I will not take a holiday again on market-day."

"Oh, go, go! and God bless you!" said good Mr. Isaacs, twinkling his eyes.

Reynolds had forgotten that he had never actually declared his love to Marianne; he fancied that she knew it as well as he did; and, perhaps, after all, she was not very much astonished when he rushed into the room and clasped her in his arms. What a joyful meeting it was! There was nevertheless a great deal which was both painful and sad to be talked over.

Reynolds, like all the rest of the world, was prepared to see an almost divine creature in Mademoiselle Angela, and she equalled his expectations.

" I do not know how it is," said Reynolds, "but she reminds me of a young actress that Williams knew in former days."·

" I think it is she," said Marianne. Of their conjectures, however, they wisely said not a word.

Marianne was two months with Mademoiselle Angela, and then Reynolds, having put his house in order to receive a wife, they were married. Mademoiselle Angela gave the breakfast, and even accompanied the bride to church. It made quite a stir in Utcceter, that Mr. Reynolds had married a *protégée* of the celebrated actress.

" But," said Miss Kendricks zealously to all their friends, "she is no actress herself, and never had anything to do with players. There can only be on Mademoiselle Angela in the world."

Within three months after the marriage, the poor

father died. Reynolds, who had never communicated his own and his sister's marriage to Williams, wrote to him now with the news of his father's death; the letter, however, reached Florence exactly two days after the Williams's had left there for England—why we shall see.

The Williams's had now been twelve months in Florence. He continued as melancholy as ever; at times he spoke of returning to England alone, but of that his wife would not hear. She urged him to consult physicians, but he, who knew too well what was his malady, would take no physician's advice. His wife now began to suspect some concealed grief or other, some sorrow of which he spared her the knowledge from affection and tenderness. "Oh, how you mistake me, Edward," she said, "if you think I cannot share in your grief!" Her affection pained him deeply—he believed that there was a grief which she could not bear—the grief of his falsehood and deceit. He avoided his wife as much as possible, and spent his time alone. All his passion for Mademoiselle Angela was gone; his wife was in his eyes a superior being, and he coveted only her love, and could he have felt that he deserved her love, he would have been the happiest of men; but he had deceived her, and in deceiving her, had compelled himself to the cruellest neglect of his father and sister. These thoughts never left him.

One day his wife drove out with the nurse and child; they went out for the day, and according to Mrs. Williams's custom, took with them provisions for every possible want. One of the pockets of the carriage was stuffed with biscuits for the child; the nurse fed him from them, and the child finding how good they were was never satisfied with them; when she thought that he had had enough, she took the cakes out and said, "Now he might have everything he could find there." Down went the little fat hand, but there was not much to find, and still the little fellow kept groping down, in the hope that there might yet be something; at last, up he brought a crumpled piece of paper—a closely crumpled letter, which seemed to have lain there a long time. His mother saw it—a letter in a female hand—it excited her curiosity; she took it and read it. She read it, looked hurriedly at the address, grew pale, and carefully folding it up put it in her reticule. She called to the coachman, and bade him turn back; she had altered her mind, and would go no farther that day.

The boy laughed and prattled on the homeward drive, but his mother neither heard nor saw him. A terrible secret had been revealed to her, and she could think of nothing but that.

On her return home she shut herself in her chamber; her husband was out on one of his hasty rides, and she re-read the letter. It was that letter which had been lost, that heart-breaking letter from Marianne to her brother. All was now clear to his wife. Her husband was then in reality the son of that unfortunate convict, Edwards—he did not bear his proper name—her child was descended from such a parentage. That might be galling to a proud spirit, but it was nothing to the cruel sense that she had been deceived, wilfully and deliberately deceived by her husband; and then that he had suffered these unfortunate relatives to suffer want—to die, perhaps

—perhaps had driven them to crime through his falsehood.

"Edward," said she sternly to him, on his return, "why have you dealt treacherously by me?"

He turned deadly pale, and sank in a chair. She spread the letter before him.

"Why have you deceived me?" she asked. "Oh, Edward, that we should have lived thus long together and you not have the candour to tell me the truth!"

He raised his eyes from the paper to her face, but said not a word.

"You have done very unkindly by me," said she, "and it is time now that we understood one another. This is no light thing, Edward, it is a grave sin before both God and man. To-morrow I leave you!"

He started up, and clasping both his hands together pressed them tightly on his forehead, "Leave me!" repeated he, in a voice of heart-rending agony.

"Yes, Edward," she said, with stern calmness, "leave you, and seek out these unhappy relatives whom you have cast off!"

"Angel of God!" exclaimed he, falling at her feet; "oh, that you could only look into my heart —could have looked into it long ago—could have known only the anguish I have endured—the punishment which I have suffered."

"But," said she, "you have let your father and sister want—your own flesh and blood—and you, yourself, have lived in case and plenty! God Almighty grant that the sorrow you have brought upon your own parent may not be visited upon you!"

She sank upon her knees beside her husband, and

bowing down her face, prayed earnestly, though without words.

They both rose from their knees. His wife laid her hand in his, and looking in his face with an expression of the most undying love, said, in a low voice, " In joy and in sorrow, in good and in evil, I am ever thine! Let us go together, and retrieve the wrong that has been done—and so may the Almighty bless us !"

He bowed his face to her hand, and wetted it with tears.

THE END.